征服考場

英文閱讀

English Reading

Michael Yang 一 著

得分王

用「抓補法」速效解題技巧，
戰勝克漏字及閱讀測驗！

User's Guide 使用說明

大量閱讀文章＋三步驟「抓補法」解題技巧，
即能攻克各大考占比分高的「克漏字」、「閱讀測驗」兩大題型，
突破英文閱讀難關，輕鬆拿分。

1 多元化文章主題，適應不同考試重點

全書共 45 回短篇、長篇文章，主
題涵蓋奇聞軼事、環保科學、歷史
文化、醫學常識……除適用不同考
試方向，更兼具趣味性，提升主動
學習興趣，備考更有效率。

06 瀕臨絕跡的白犀牛
The Endangered Rhinoceros
07 地球暖化的危機
The Global Warming crisis
08 額外的假期
The Additional Holiday
09 奇蹟寶寶
A Babe of Miracle
10 生命奇蹟
Miracle of Life
11 美國失業率
America's Lowest Unemployment Rate
12 醫學的進展
The Advancement in Medicine
13 著作權
Copyright
14 成功的關鍵 078
The Key to Success
15 偶像的魅力 083

07 無限畸型症 152
Amplification
08 尊嚴死法案 158
The "Death with Dignity" Law
09 沒整理的床有助健康 164
Unmade Beds may Keep You Healthy
10 穿腦雷達 170
Zongti II
11 網路大數據的應用 176
The Application of Network Big Data
12 時尚派對邀請 182
Fashion Party Invitation
13 物聯網 188
The Internet of Things
14 地質學家的工作 194
What Does a Geologist Do?
15 給 Sobo 族的建議 200
Some Suggestions for "Sobo"
16 法律的目的 206
The Purpose of Law
17 旅行的捷徑 212
The Short Cut of Travel
18 壓力對健康的影響 218
How does Stress Influence Our Health
19 經理人的責任 224
A Manager's Responsibility
20 山寨效應 230
The "Shanzhai" Effect
21 職場社交 237

17 旅行的捷徑
The Short Cut of Travel
18 壓力對健康的影響

2 大量測驗練習，考前全力衝刺

20 回克漏字＋ 25 回閱讀測驗，內
容由淺入深；只要勤作練習，熟悉
兩大重要題型後，不論是平時備考
或短期衝刺，都能掌握考題方向，
輕鬆應考。

"Employment gains have been modest in recent months, so in
that sense I think businesses that were initially very wary of taking
on permanent full-time employees are feeling more confident
now than some months ago," said Richard DeKaser, an economist
Parthenon Group in Boston. "___(5)___ they are more willing to
make those kinds of long-term commitments."

___ 01. (A) by   (B) at   (C) in   (D) on
___ 02. (A) under   (B) on   (C) of   (D) in
___ 03. (A) and it add   (B) and adding   (C) adding   (D) added
___ 04. (A) appearing   (B) declining   (C) increasing
        (D) disciplining
___ 05. (A) Result in   (B) As a result   (C) On the contrary
        (D) As a whole

fixed all the petty problems will gain you m...
improve your concentration. Thus, you are giv...
point to overcome the bigger issues in your l...
flexible, look at problems from different an...
onto the stresses that you can't control over, ...
stresses that you do have control over. At the e...
that the anxiety and depression is uncontrollab...
physicians or professional organizations.

___ 01. Which of the following factors was not mentioned as the cause
        of stresses in the article?
        (A) unmanageable pressures   (B) anxieties of modern life
        (C) worries   (D) bad living conditions
___ 02. When we are _____, we can feel our muscles are
        stiff, our brains are shattered, and our tempers are short.
        (A) stressed   (B) happy   (C) nervous   (D) frightened
___ 03. Referring to the text, one of the best ways to alleviate stress is to
        _____.
        (A) do exercises   (B) eat food
        (C) list "Trivial" and "Serious" issues   (D) shout loudly

3 「抓補法」解題三步驟，答題快速準確

不論文章程度深淺，內容長短，搭配「抓補法」解題方式：1 先抓頭、2 再抓尾、3 善用補強關鍵，簡單三個動作，即可迅速找出正確答案；熟能生巧，高分在握。

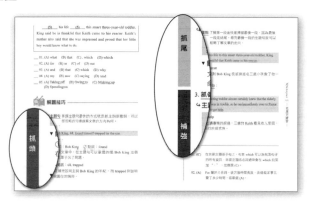

4 精萃解析，統整文法概念，提升英文能力

精選生難字詞及重要的文法解析，適合高中程度以上的英文學習者；不僅能助釐清易混淆觀念，還能延伸學習更多關鍵句型、文法，快速理解題型，提升閱讀能力。

Preface 作者序

大家都知道,「克漏字測驗」及「閱讀測驗」已成為目前各大英語重要考試的必考題型了,而且所占比分高;同時,這兩項測驗在解題時,必須對照上下文意,與傳統單題式的解題技巧大不相同,屬於一種全方位綜合性的測驗。

可惜的是,在台灣部分的學生在平日裡累積了不錯的單字力,一旦遇到這兩大題型,卻是一籌莫展。但真的那麼困難嗎?其實比較起來,在各大重要考試裡,閱讀測驗反倒是較容易拿分的部分,只要能抓到解題技巧,並且多作練習,即能發揮原有的單字力,即使看不懂全文,也能輕易拿分。

所以這一回我特別網羅不同的各種主題文章共 45 回,包含克漏字 20 回以及閱讀測驗 25 回,就是希望讓大家藉由不斷地大量練習,能熟悉題型,克服考試恐懼。

特別要強調的是:藉由在寫練習題中,我也將平時帶領學生們有效的解題技巧—「抓補法」,分享給讀者們,只要三個動作:1 抓頭、2 抓尾、3 關鍵補強,即能輕鬆理解文意,快速找出正確答案;藉由大量的測驗練習解題,不僅熟悉解題技巧,也能快速、輕鬆地輕取高分。

全書的文章程度,由淺入深,對於正在準備全民英檢中級、英檢中高級、學測、指考等重要考試的考生們都大有幫助,只要配合「抓補法」的解題方式勤於練習,相信即使是在有限的時間內,也能在家輕鬆練功,順利拿下理想地成績!

Contents 目錄

👋 Chapter 1 克漏字練習

01 家庭悲劇 ——————— 008
A Family Accident

02 轉世化身 ——————— 013
Reincarnation

03 良好睡眠條件 ——————— 018
Tips for a Good Night's Sleep

04 聰明的三歲孩子 ——————— 023
A Clever Three-year hyphen old Toddler

05 動物權利 ——————— 028
Animal Rights

06 瀕臨絕跡的白犀牛 ——————— 033
The Endangered white Rhinoceros

07 地球暖化的危機 ——————— 038
The Global Warming crisis

08 額外的假期 ——————— 044
The Additional Holiday

09 奇蹟寶寶 ——————— 050
A Baby of Miracle

10 生命奇蹟 ——————— 055
Miracle of Life

11 美國失業率 ——————— 060
America's Lowest Unemployment Rate

12 醫學的進展 ——————— 066
The Advances in Medicine

13 著作權 ——————— 072
Copyright

14 成功的關鍵 ——————— 078
The Key to Success

15 倫敦的魅力 ——————— 083
The Charm of London

16 健康飲食 ——————— 088
Healthy Diet

17 共同資金 ——————— 094
Mutual Funds

18 信用評價的重要 ——————— 100
The Importance of Credit Rating

19 人事管理政策 ——————— 105
Personnel Management Policy

20 流冰 V.S. 生態 ——————— 111
Shifting Ice V.S. Environment

👋 Chapter 2 閱讀測驗

01 愛的禮物 ——————— 120
The Gift of Love

02 死而復生的貓 ——————— 125
The Cat that Came Back to Life

03 錄取通知 ——————— 130
Admission Notice

04 被破壞的尼加拉瓜湖 ——————— 135
The Destructed Lake Nicaragua

05 東京南方海域升起的火山 —— 140
Erupting Island Rises from South of Tokyo

06 月亮離地球愈來愈遠 ——————— 146
The Moon is Moving Further fram Earth

07 無眼畸型症 ——————— 152
Anophthalmia

08 尊嚴死法案 ——————— 158
The "Death with Dignity" Law

09 沒整理的床有助健康 ——————— 164
Unmade Beds may Keep You Healthy

10 穿牆雷達 ——————— 170
Range-R

11 網路大數據的應用 ——————— 176
The Application of Network: Big Data

12 時尚派對邀請 ——————— 182
Fashion Party Invitation

13 物聯網 ——————— 188
The Internet of Things

14 地質學家的工作 ——————— 194
What Does a Geologist Do?

15 給 Soho 族的建議 ——————— 200
Some Suggestions for "Soho"

16 法律的目的 ——————— 206
The Purpose of Law

17 旅行的捷徑 ——————— 212
The Short Cut of Travel

18 壓力對健康的影響 ——————— 218
How does Stress Influence Our Health

19 經理人的責任 ——————— 224
A Manager's Responsibility

20 山寨效應 ——————— 230
The "Shanzhai" Effect

21 職場社交 ——————— 237
Social Activities at Work

22 強迫症 ——————— 244
The OCD Symptoms

23 談「視訊會議」 ——————— 251
On "Video Conferencing"

24 良好的談判技巧 ——————— 258
The Good Negotiation Skill

25 真正的天堂 ——————— 265
The Real Heaven

Chapter 1.

克漏字
練習

理解段落文意後，將挖空的部分，
補上缺漏的正確字詞。

A Family Accident

A 29-year-old mother was accidentally shot and killed by her two-year-old boy ___(1)___ she was shopping in a Walmart store in Hayden, Idaho at about 10:20 a.m. local time on Tuesday. According to the police, the toddler was sitting at the front of the shopping cart when he found a gun ___(2)___ in his mother's handbag and accidentally fired the licensed gun.

The Kootenai county sheriff office's spokesman, Stu Miller, said that the 29-year-old mother, Veronica Rutledge, who was from Blackfoot in southeastern Idaho and was visiting relatives in the area, had a permit of concealed weapons.

Several store employees witnessed the shooting while the whole accident was captured on surveillance video. The shooting happened near the store's electronics section. The toddler reached into his mother's purse and grabbed a ___(3)___ small caliber handgun, which discharged ___(4)___ .

Police determined that the shooting was accidental after ___(5)___ the store video. "It appears to be a pretty tragic accident," Miller said.

___ 01. (A) what   (B) which   (C) how   (D) when

___ 02. (A) concealed   (B) sealed   (C) advanced   (D) satisfied

___ 03. (A) hide   (B) hid   (C) hiding   (D) hidden

___ 04. (A) again　(B) one　(C) once　(D) occasionally

___ 05. (A) review　(B) reviewing　(C) reviewed　(D) reviews

 解題技巧 ──────────────────

抓頭

1. **抓主題句** 掌握主題句最快的方式就是抓主詞跟動詞，可以很粗略的知道這篇文章的方向為何。

↳ 主題句：

> A 29-year-old <u>mother</u> was accidentally <u>shot and killed</u> by her two-year-old boy when she was shopping in a Walmart store in Hayden, Idaho.

▼ 關鍵字：

① 主詞：mother　② 動詞：shot and killed

在這篇文章中，從主題句可以掌握到本文的重點是一名母親遭到槍殺。

▼ 其他資訊：

by her 2-year-old boy 是補充說明母親遭到兩歲親生兒子槍殺。

抓尾

2. **抓末段重點** 了解第一段後快速掃描最後一段，因為最後一段是結尾，看完最後一段的主題句就可以粗略了解文章的走向。

↳ 主題句：

> Police determined that the shooting was <u>accidental</u> after reviewing the store video.

▼ 關鍵字：accidental

文章末段提到警方確認這起開槍事件是意外。

3. 抓各段的主題句：

↳ 主題句：

> Several store employees witnessed the shooting while the whole <u>accident</u> was captured on surveillance video.

▼ 關鍵字：accident

這一段在講整起意外被錄影監視器拍攝下來，能看出目擊的店員也認為這是一場意外。

解析

01. **(D)** when 為連接詞，連接兩連續動作，故答案為 (D)。

02. **(A)** **(A) 隱藏**、(B) 密封、(C) 先進的、(D) 滿足的，由文章可知，背包藏有一把槍，故選 concealed，答案為 (A)。

03. **(D)** hidden 是 hide 的過去分詞，過去分詞是用來表示「已完成的動作」，答案選 (D)。

04. **(C)** once 可作副詞、連接詞和名詞，當副詞時，有「一次」的意思，也可代表「曾經」，依據文章此手槍曾被使用一次，故選 once 答案為 (C)。

05. **(B)** After 是代表時間的連接詞，意思是「在……之後」，省略主詞時，後方可加 V-ing，故應選 reviewing，答案為 (B)。

必學詞彙

> » **shoot** v. 射擊；開槍
> » **toddler** n. 學步的小孩
> » **shopping cart**
>   n. 購物推車
> » **conceal**
>   v. 隱蔽；隱瞞；隱藏
>
> » **licensed**
>   adj. 得到許可的
> » **discharge**
>   v.（槍砲等）發射
> » **accidental**
>   adj. 意外的；偶然的

文法觀念

1. The toddler reached into his mother's purse and grabbed a hidden small caliber handgun, **which** discharged **once**.

   • hidden 是 hide 的過去分詞，在此形容手槍為「隱藏式」，例：The police found a little boy hidden in the bushes. 警方找到一名躲在樹叢裡的小男孩。

   • which 是關係代名詞，用來引導關係子句，修飾前面的先行詞，例：This is the story which Mr. Poe wrote. 這是波先生寫的故事，Mr. Poe wrote 修飾 the story。

   • once 可作副詞、連接詞和名詞。當副詞時，有「一次」的意思，也可代表「曾經」，例：I was once a waitress. 我曾經是一名服務生。

2. Police determined that the shooting was accidental **after** reviewing the store video. "It appears to be a pretty tragic accident," Miller said.

   • After 是代表時間的連接詞，意思是「在……之後」，省略主詞時，後方可加 V-ing，例：After receiving the bag, I will send you the money. 收到包包之後，我會匯錢給你。

家庭悲劇

一名二十九歲的母親，在當地時間星期二上午 10 點 20 分左右，在愛達荷州海登市的一家沃爾瑪超市逛街時，意外被她兩歲的兒子開槍射死。根據警方表示，這名學步娃兒當時是坐在購物推車前方，發現了藏在他媽媽手提包裡這把有執照的手槍，並不小心開槍。

庫特內縣警長辦公室發言人史都米勒說，這位是二十九歲母親維若妮卡羅特雷，從愛達荷州布南部萊克福市來這區拜訪親戚的，她持有隱藏式武器許可證。

有幾個店員目擊了這起射擊事件，而整起意外也被錄影監視器拍攝下來。這起射擊意外是發生在該店的電子用品區附近。這名學步兒伸手進他媽媽的包包，抓出了一把藏在包包裡的小口徑手槍，並且射擊了一次。

警方在看過店家的錄影帶後，確認這起開槍事件是個意外。「這顯然是個相當悲慘的意外！」米勒說。

Reincarnation

Luke Ruehlman, a five-year-old boy from Cincinnati, Ohio, claims to remember his previous life, saying that he was a 30-year-old black woman who died in a house fire. After ___**(1)**___ her boy's story, Luke's mother Erika is convinced that his references were being made to a real woman called Pamela Robinson ___**(2)**___ died when the Paxton Hotel caught fire in Chicago in 1993.

___**(3)**___ Erika, Luke began to make references to the woman at the age of two. At first he simply named things Pam, then started referring to when he "used to be a girl," she said. He used to say, "When I was a girl, I had black hair" or

"I ___**(4)**___ have earrings like that when I was a girl." Moreover, Luke even ___**(5)**___ being reincarnated and recalls being named by his parents. Erica said that her boy claimed he used to be Pam, "but I died. I went up to heaven, and I saw God, and he pushed me back down and when I woke up, I was a baby and you named me Luke."

___ 01. (A) reseacher　(B) reseached　(C) reseaching　(D) reseaches

___ 02. (A) when　(B) who　(C) what　(D) which

___ 03. (A) In additon to　(B) According to　(C) Accordingly
　　　(D) Additionally

___ 04. (A) used　(B) was used to　(C) used to　(D) was using

___ 05. (A) recollects　(B) collects　(C) reminds　(D) forgets

解題技巧

抓
頭

1. **抓主題句** 掌握主題句最快的方式就是抓主詞跟動詞，可以很粗略的知道這篇文章的方向為何。

↳ 主題句：

> Luke Ruehlman, a five-year-old boy from Cincinnati, Ohio, claims to remember his previous life.

▼ 關鍵字：

① 主詞：Luke Ruehlman　② 動詞：claims
在這篇文章中，從主題句可以掌握的是 Luke 宣稱自己記得前世。

▼ 其他資訊：five-year-old, Cincinnati, Ohio

five-year-old, Cincinnati, Ohio 是補充說明主詞 Luke Ruehlman 的年紀和居住地。

2. **抓末段重點** 了解第一段後快速掃描最後一段，因為最後一段是結尾，看完最後一段的主題句就可以粗略了解文章的走向。

↳ 主題句：

抓
尾

> Luke even recollects being reincarnated and recollects being named by his parents.

▼ 關鍵字：recollects

文章末段提到 Luke 能回憶自己轉世的情況，和出生時父母替他取名的過程。

補強

3. **抓各段的主題句**：

↳ 主題句：

> According to Erika, Luke began to make <u>references</u> to the woman at the age of two.

▼ 關鍵字：references

這一段在講 Luke 從兩歲就開始提起這件事，同樣能看出 Luke 認為自己前世是一名女子。

解析

01. **(C)** 當兩個句子「主詞相同」時，為精簡句子並變化句型就可使用「分詞構句」。且依文意將 "she researched" 簡化為 V-ing 分詞構句，故應選 researching，答案為 (C)。

02. **(B)** who 是關係代名詞，替代先行詞 Pamela Robinson，來引導關係子句，並修飾所替代的先行詞，答案應選 (B)。

03. **(B)** (A) 此外、**(B) 根據**、(C) 於是、(D) 另外，只有 according to 符合文意，故答案應選 (B)。

04. **(C)** 用來表示過去經常做，但現在不再出現的行為。Used to 裡的 to 是不定詞，因此後方接原型動詞 used to + V，答案應選 (C)。

05. **(A)** **(A) 回想**、(B) 收集、(C) 提醒、(D) 忘記，根據文章，小男孩回憶前世記憶，故應選 recollect，答案應選 (A)。

必學詞彙

> » **previous** life **n.** 前世
> » **convince**
>   **v.** 使確信；使信服
> » **reference**
>   **n.** 提及；涉及
> » **recollect** **v.** 回想；追憶
>
> » **reincarnate**
>   **v.** 使化身；使轉世
> » **recall** **v.** 回憶；回想
> » **heaven**
>   **n.** 天堂；天國；上帝

文法觀念

1. According to Erika, Luke began to make references to the woman at the age of two.

   • According to 為常見的片語，是「根據」的意思，後方通常接人名或名詞，例：If everything goes according to plan, we will be home by 5. 如果一切按計畫進行，我們 5 點會到家。

   • → The age of 表示年齡，常見的片語 at the age of... 意思是「某人幾歲時」，例：I started learning German at the age of 18. 我 18 歲開始學德文。

2. At first he simply named things Pam, then started referring to when he "**used to** be a girl," she said. He **used to** say, "When I was a girl, I had black hair" or "I **used to** have earrings like that when I was a girl."

   • used to 用來表示過去經常做，但現在不再出現的行為。used to 裡的 to 是不定詞，因此後方接原型動詞 used to + V，例如：He doesn't love me like he used to. 他不像過去那樣愛我。

轉世化身

　　美國俄亥俄州辛辛那提市的五歲男童路克盧曼，聲稱記得自己的前世，說自己是死於一場大火的三十歲黑人女性。對兒子所說的話做過調查後，路克的母親愛莉卡深信他所指的，是一名真實存在過的女性，在 1993 年芝加哥派斯頓酒店的一場大火中喪命的潘蜜拉羅賓森。

　　愛莉卡說，路克在兩歲的時候就開始提起這名女子的事。她說：「一開始他只是會把東西取名為潘，然後就開始說自己『曾經是個女孩』。」他曾經說：「當我是個女孩時，我有一頭黑髮。」或是「當我是個女孩時，我曾經戴過像那樣的耳環。」

　　除此之外，路克甚至能想起自己轉世的過程，以及被爸媽取名字的事。愛莉卡說她兒子說他自己曾經是潘，「但是後來我死了。我上了天堂，看到了上帝，然後他又把我推下來。當我醒的時候，我是個小寶寶，你們把我取名為路克。」

03

Tips for a Good Night's Sleep

Getting a good night's sleep is a vital indicator of overall health. Lack of sleep can not only make us space out during the day, __(1)__ increase our __(2)__ depression, anxiety, and other diseases.

But how much sleep do we really need? While eight hours has long been the golden standard for adults, an expert panel of scientists and sleep specialists believe that the largest single factor that affects sleep __(3)__ is age.

According to the National Sleep Foundation (NSF), children, particularly babies, need __(4)__ more sleep than adults. While 0-3 month newborns need 14-17 hours of sleep each day and school age children need 9-11 hours, adults aged above 18 only need 7-9 hours.

Younger children have a much higher arousal threshold __(5)__ allows them to sleep through even quite loud noises and helps them to achieve the long sleep periods they need. While the elderly need just as much sleep as younger adults, their night sleep is lighter, shorter, and more fragmented, so they have to take afternoon naps.

___ 01. (A) also   (B) but also   (C) else   (D) and

___ 02. (A) consist of   (B) lack of   (C) risk of   (D) use of

___ 03. (A) management   (B) requirements   (C) attainments
       (D) disappointments

___ 04. (A) much   (B) many   (C) very   (D) so

___ 05. (A) , which   (B) and   (C) so   (D) what

 解題技巧 ——————————

抓頭

1. **抓主題句** 掌握主題句最快的方式就是抓主詞跟動詞，可以很粗略的知道這篇文章的方向為何。

↳ 主題句：

> Getting a good night's sleep <u>is</u> a vital indicator of <u>overall health</u>.

▼ 關鍵字：

① 主詞：overall health   ② 動詞：is

在這篇文章中，從主題句可以掌握到文章主題是健康和睡眠。

抓尾

2. **抓末段重點** 了解第一段後快速掃描最後一段，因為最後一段是結尾，看完最後一段的主題句就可以粗略了解文章的走向。

↳ 主題句：

> Younger children have a much <u>higher arousal threshold</u> that allows them to sleep through even quite loud noises and helps them to achieve the long sleep periods they need.

▼ 關鍵字：higher arousal threshold

→ 文章末段提到孩童在較大的噪音中也能睡覺，可以看出文章在講睡眠與年紀之間的關係。

3. **抓各段的主題句：**

↳ 主題句：

> An expert panel of scientists and sleep specialists believe that the largest single factor that affects sleep requirements is <u>age</u>.

▼ 關鍵字：age

這一段在講科學家認為影響所需睡眠最大的因素就是年齡。

 解析

01. **(B)**   Not only...but also... 為對等連接詞，意思是「不僅……也是……」。兩邊的詞性與時態必須對稱、相等，故答案為 (B)。

02. **(C)**   (A) 包括、(B) 缺乏、**(C) 風險**、(D) 用於，根據文章，缺乏睡眠會增加我們罹患沮喪、焦慮和其他疾病的風險，故選 risk of，答案為 (C)。

03. **(B)**   (A) 管理、**(B) 需求**、(C) 素養、(D) 失望。

04. **(A)**   副詞或形容詞變成比較級時，通常可被 much、far、a lot、a great deal、still、even 等六個副詞修飾，故選 much，答案為 (A)。

05. **(A)**   , which 是關係代名詞，替代先行詞 threshold，用來引導<u>關係子句</u>，並修飾所替代的先行詞，答案應選 (A)。

 **必學詞彙**

» **vital**
  `adj.` 維持生命所必需的

» **spaced out**
  `adj.` 昏昏沉沉的

» **standard**
  `n.` 標準；水準；規格；
  規範

» **panel** `n.` 專門小組

» **requirement**
  `n.` 要求條件；需要；
  必需品

» **fragmented**
  `adj.` 不完整的；成碎片
  的

» **nap** `n.` 午睡；打盹兒

 文法觀念

1. **Lack of** sleep can **not only** make us space out during the day, but also increases our risk of depression, anxiety, and **other** diseases.

- Lack of，lack 在此為名詞，Lack 當名詞時，後面固定搭配介系詞 of，例：Don't put off applying for your dream job just for your lack of work experience. 別因為缺乏工作經驗就不敢去爭取你夢想中的工作。

- Not only...but also... 為對等連接詞，意思是「不僅……也是……」兩邊的詞性與時態必須對稱、相等，例：He is not only kind but also handsome. 他不僅人好還很帥。

- Other 可作代名詞，也可以作為限定詞，後方接不可數名詞或複數名詞，若後方接了單數名詞，other 的前方必須加上另一個限定詞，例：The other dog at the park didn't like strangers at all. 公園裡的另一隻狗非常不喜歡陌生人。

 **中文翻譯**

良好睡眠條件

擁有一夜好眠對整體健康是個重要的指標。缺乏睡眠不僅會讓我們白天時感到昏昏沉沉，也會增加我們罹患沮喪、焦慮和其他疾病的風險。

但是我們究竟需要多少睡眠呢？雖然八小時一直都是成年人所需睡眠的黃金標準，但是一個由科學家及睡眠專家組成的專業小組認為，影響所需睡眠的最重要因素，就是年齡。

美國國家睡眠基金會表示，孩童，特別是嬰兒，需要比成年人更多的睡眠。0-3 個月的新生兒每天需要 14-17 個小時的睡眠，學齡兒童需要 9-11 小時的睡眠，而 18 歲以上的成年人則只需要 7-9 小時。

越小的孩子越不容易被喚醒，這使得他們能夠在非常大聲的噪音中保持熟睡，從而讓他們能獲得他們所需要的長時間睡眠。雖然老年人跟青年人需要一樣多的睡眠，但他們夜間睡眠較淺、較短也不完整，因此他們必須靠午休來補足睡眠時間。

04

A Clever Three-year hyphen old Toddler

Bob King, 68, found himself trapped in the car, __(1)__ apparently had an electrical issue that caused the doors to lock up. He was unable to get out of it after trying hard __(2)__ close to five minutes.

It was 32.7 degrees Celsius outside that day, and the temperature inside the vehicle had reached over 48.8 degrees Celsius. King was seized with panic, and it was at this moment __(3)__ he spotted 3-year-old Keith Williams walking past the car. He knocked on the car window to stop the toddler and gestured him to help him out.

The fast-acting toddler almost certainly knew that the elderly inside the car was in trouble, so he ran immediately over to Pastor Jack Greene to get help. "Little Keith came behind me and kept __(4)__ , Locked, locked, locked," Greene said. Then Keith started patting and pulling his hand, and kept saying, "hot, hot." So, Greene followed

Keith out and saw Bob in the car. Greene then opened the car door with all his might and saved the elderly before he was dehydrated.

___**(5)**___ his life ___**(5)**___ this smart three-year-old toddler, King said he is thankful that Keith came to his rescue. Keith's mother also said that she was impressed and proud that her little boy would know what to do.

___ 01. (A) what   (B) that   (C) , which   (D) which
___ 02. (A) for   (B) in   (C) of   (D) out
___ 03. (A) and   (B) that   (C) which   (D) why
___ 04. (A) say   (B) saw   (C) saying   (D) said
___ 05. (A) Taking;off   (B) Owing;to   (C) Making;up
     (D) Spending;on

 解題技巧 ━━━━━━━━━━━━━━━━━━━━

抓
頭

1. **抓主題句** 掌握主題句最快的方式就是抓主詞跟動詞,可以很粗略的知道這篇文章的方向為何。

↳ 主題句:

> Bob King, 68, found himself trapped in the car.

▼ 關鍵字:

① 主詞:Bob King   ② 動詞:found
在這篇文章中,從主題句可以掌握的是 Bob King 這個人發現車子出了問題。

▼ 其他資訊:68, trapped
68 是補充說明主詞 Bob King 的年紀,而 trapped 則說明他被困住的情形。

2. **抓末段重點** 了解第一段後快速掃描最後一段,因為最後
　　　　　　　一段是結尾,看完最後一段的主題句就可以
　　　　　　　粗略了解文章的走向。

↳ 主題句:

抓尾

> Owing his life to this smart three-year-old toddler, King said he is thankful that Keith came to his <u>rescue</u>.

▼ 關鍵字:rescue

文章末段提到 Bob King 很感謝這名三歲小孩救了他一命。

3. **抓各段的主題句**:

↳ 主題句:

補強

> The fast-acting toddler almost certainly knew that the elderly inside the car was in trouble, so he ran immediately over to Pastor Jack Greene to get <u>help</u>.

▼ 關鍵字:help

這一段在講事情的經過,三歲的 Keith 看見老人受困,機靈地去找牧師求救。

 解析

01. **(C)**　在非限定關係子句上,句首 which 可以指前面句子的所有資訊,非限定關係名詞通常會在 which 前面加 " , " ,故應選 (C)。

02. **(A)**　For 屬於介系詞,後方接時間長度,表達做某事花費了多少時間,答案選 (A)。

Chapter 01 ── 克漏字練習 ──

03. **(B)** 分裂句的功能為加強語氣，將強調的部分放在主詞補語（it）的位置，It+is / was+N / 片語 +that...，答案為 (B)。

04. **(C)** keep 後通常接 V-ing，故選 (C)。

05. **(B)** (A) 拖掉、**(B) 虧欠**、(C) 化妝、(D) 花費，文中老人受幼童拯救，故可說老人欠幼童一條命，答案應選 (B)。

 ## 必學詞彙

> **trap** v. 困住；設陷阱

> **lock** v. 鎖住；鎖上

> **temperature** n. 氣溫；溫度

> **panic** n. 驚慌；恐慌

> **toddler** n. 學步的孩子

> **dehydrated** adj. 脫水的

> **rescue** n. 救援；營救

 ## 文法觀念

1. <u>Bob King, 68, **found** himself **trapped** in the car, which apparently had an electrical issue that caused the doors to lock up, and was unable to get out of it after trying hard for close to five minutes.</u>

   • Found...trapped 的用法，found 在此是「發現」的意思，發現某人⋯⋯後方加過去分詞或形容詞表示狀態，例：A 60-year-old man reported missing from Peru has been found alive. 一名據報在祕魯失蹤的 60 歲男子被發現生還。

   • For 屬於介系詞，後方接時間長度，表達某事持續了多少時間，I have known him for 25 years. 我已經認識他 25 年了。

2. The **fast-acting** toddler almost certainly knew that the elderly inside the car was in trouble, so he ran immediately over to Pastor Jack Greene to get help.

- Fast-acting 屬於複合形容詞，複合形容詞有許多型態，此為形容詞－現在分詞的用法，例如：good-looking 好看的、English-speaking 說英文的、long-lasting 持久的、thought-provoking 刺激思考的、time-saving 省時的。

中文翻譯

聰明的三歲孩子

　　六十八歲的鮑勃金恩，發現自己被困在車門因電子問題而上鎖的車內，而且在努力嘗試近五分鐘之後，依然無法離開車子。

　　那天外頭氣溫是攝氏 32.7 度，而車內的溫度超過攝氏 48.8 度。就在金恩驚慌失措時，他發現三歲的基斯威廉斯走過。他敲車窗，讓這個學步娃停下來，並用手勢要他幫他出去。

　　這個反應很快的學步娃幾乎很確切地知道車子內的老人有麻煩了，所以他立刻跑去向牧師傑克葛林恩求助。

　　「小基斯走到我身後，不斷說著：『鎖住了，鎖住了，鎖住了！』」葛林恩說。接著基斯開始拍打並拉他的手，不斷說：「熱，熱。」於是葛林恩便跟著基斯出去，並看到鮑勃在車子裡。葛林恩用盡全力拉開車門，並在這位老翁脫水之前將他救出來。

　　金恩可以說是欠這個聰明的三歲學步娃一條命。他說，他很感謝基斯來救他。基斯的母親也表示，她的兒子知道該怎麼做，她感到很感動，也很驕傲。

05

Animal Rights

An overweight man climbed into a pen at a Spanish Christmas market and sat on a new-born donkey to pose for a photo on 10 December. Two days later, local residents noticed the small donkey could barely stand, and it died the next morning because of severe __(1)__ injuries.

The picture, which shows an obese man sat on the donkey's back and adopted a "galloping" pose, was widely __(2)__ online. It is alleged that the poor donkey was __(3)__ to death. Local animal rights activists in Lucena, Andalusia, said the injuries were like the "insides burst," and the donkey had spent three days in "agony" before it died.

__(4)__ the traditional live nativity scene is always a huge feature of Christmas in Lucena, Andalusia, the tiny five-month-old donkey, named Platero, was not meant to be ridden as part of the Christmas scene in the town.

The police investigation follows complaints from the Association for the Defence of Donkeys and Lucena Animal Circle. Animal rights campaigners in Spain have also called for the use of live animals in nativity scenes to be banned __(5)__ the incident.

___ 01. (A) horrible   (B) international   (C) internal   (D) remarkable

___ 02. (A) circulate   (B) circulating   (C) circulated   (D) circulates

___ 03. (A) squashed　　(B) crushed　　(C) refused　　(D) injected

___ 04. (A) What　　(B) While　　(C) Which　　(D) Whatever

___ 05. (A) follow　　(B) following　　(C) followed　　(D) follow up

 解題技巧 ───────────

抓頭

1. **抓主題句** 掌握主題句最快的方式就是抓主詞跟動詞，可以很粗略的知道這篇文章的方向為何。

↳ 主題句：

> 　　Two days later, local residents noticed the small donkey could barely stand, and it died the next morning because of severe internal injuries.

▼ 關鍵字：

① 主詞：the small donkey　　② 動詞：died

在這篇文章中，從主題句可以掌握的是小驢子和死亡。

▼ 其他資訊：

severe internal injuries 是補充說明小驢子死亡的原因。

抓尾

2. **抓末段重點** 了解第一段後快速掃描最後一段，因為最後一段是結尾，看完最後一段的主題句就可以粗略了解文章的走向。

↳ 主題句：

> 　　The police investigation follows complaints from the Association for the Defence of Donkeys and Lucena Animal Circle.

▼ 關鍵字：investigation

文章末段提到經過動保團體的投訴，警方目前正在調查此案。

3. **抓各段的主題句：**

↳ 主題句：

> Local animal rights activists in Lucena, Andalusia, said the injuries were like the "insides burst," and the donkey had spent three days in "agony" before it died.

▼ 關鍵字：“insides burst”

這一段在講驢子體內爆裂的情形，同樣能看出小驢子遭到重壓後身亡。

解析

01. **(C)**　(A) 可怕的、(B) 國際的、**(C) 內部的**、(D) 傑出的，依據文章，驢子因被胖子重壓而內傷，internal injury 為內傷，故答案選 (C)。

02. **(C)**　由於照片是被流傳，要用被動式 be +v-pp，故應選過去分詞 circulated，答案選 (C)。

03. **(A)**　**(A) 把……壓扁**、(B) 壓碎、(C) 拒絕、(D) 注射，依據文章，驢子是被胖子壓死，故選壓扁 squash，答案應選 (A)。

04. **(B)**　while 為連接詞，連接兩連續動作，故答案為 (B)。

05. **(B)**　following 在此作介系詞，指的是「在……之後」，後方接名詞，答案選 (B)。

必學詞彙

> **internal**
  adj. 內部的；內在的

> **obese**
  adj. 肥胖的；過胖的

> **circulate**
  v. 流傳；傳播；傳播

> **squash** v. 把……壓扁；擠壓

> **agony**
  n. 極度痛苦；苦惱

> **complaint**
  n. 抱怨；怨言；抗議

> **ban** v. 禁止；取締

文法觀念

1. **While** the traditional live nativity scene is **always** a huge feature of Christmas in Lucena, Andalusia, the tiny five-month-old donkey, named Platero, was not meant to be ridden as part of the Christmas scene in the town.

   • while 是連接詞，連結句子中兩個同時進行的持續性動作，例：I was out walking the dog while my mom was cooking. 媽媽在煮飯時，我在外面遛狗。

   • always 屬於頻率副詞，代表「總是」，例：Bill always buys his daughter a gift when he goes on a business trip. 比爾出差時總會買禮物給他的女兒。常用的頻率副詞還有 usually（通常），often（常常），sometimes（有時候），never（從來沒有）。

2. The police investigation follows complaints from the Association for the Defence of Donkeys and Lucena Animal Circle. Animal rights campaigners in Spain have also called for **the use of** live animals in nativity scenes to be banned **following** the incident.

- the use of 的意思是「用……」，後方接名詞，例：The use of cocaine eventually took the young singer's life. 食用古柯鹼最終奪走這名年輕歌手的性命。
- following 在此作介系詞，指的是「在……之後」，後方接名詞，例：They got divorced following the incident. 他們在這件事之後離婚了。

 **中文翻譯**

動物權利

　　十二月十日這天，一個體重過重的男子，在一個西班牙聖誕市集中爬進牲畜圍欄，並坐在一隻剛出生不久的小驢子上，擺出姿勢拍照。兩天後，當地居民發現這隻小驢子沒辦法站立，更在隔天早上因為嚴重內傷死亡。

　　肥胖男子坐在驢子背上，並擺出馳騁姿勢的照片，在網路上瘋傳。網友斷言，這隻可憐的驢子是被壓死的。安達魯西亞區盧塞納的動物權利人士表示，這隻驢子所受的傷就像從體內爆開來一樣，讓這隻驢子在死前三天經歷了極度的痛苦。

　　雖然傳統的耶穌誕生場景，一直是安達盧西亞區盧塞納聖誕節的一個重要特色。但這隻被命名「佩特拉羅」才只有五個月大的小驢子，是這小鎮的聖誕場景的一部分，而不是用來騎的。

　　在守護驢子協會及盧塞納動物團體提出抗議後，警方已經展開調查。發生這個事件後，西班牙的動物權利人士也呼籲，應該要禁止在耶穌誕生場景中使用活生生的動物。

06

The Endangered white Rhinoceros

44-year-old Angalifu, a male northern white rhinoceros, died of natural causes at the San Diego Zoo in California, leavingonly five __(1)__ northern square-lipped rhinoceroses remain on Earth.

"Angalifu's death is a __(2)__ loss to all of us," in a statement San Diego Zoo Safari Park curator Randy Rieches wrote, "Not only because he was well beloved here at the park, __(3)__ because his death brings this wonderful species one step closer to extinction."

One of the critically endangered northern white rhinos remains at the California facility, while another resides in the Czech Republic Zoo and three remain in Kenyan preserve. Right now, there is only one male rhino __(4)__ lives semi-wild at the Ol Pejeta animal park in Kenya, in the world.

San Diego Zoo's earlier attempts to mate Angalifu with the zoo's other northern white rhino, Nola, were unsuccessful. __(5)__, preservationists at the Kenyan preserve also acknowledged that their one male and two female rhinos are incapable of reproducing naturally. Vitro fertilization (IVF) efforts are now undertaken to save the species from extinction.

___ 01. (A) know   (B) known   (C) knowing   (D) knew
___ 02. (A) tremendous   (B) ridiculous   (C) monotony   (D) obious
___ 03. (A) but also   (B) also   (C) else   (D) and

___ 04. (A) when　(B) who　(C) which　(D) what

___ 05. (A) While　(B) Meanwhile　(C) Therefore　(D) Recently

 解題技巧 ─────────────────────

1. **抓主題句** 掌握主題句最快的方式就是抓主詞跟動詞，可以
　很粗略的知道這篇文章的方向為何。

↳ 主題句：

> 44-year-old Angalifu, a male northern white rhinoceros, has died of natural causes at the San Diego Zoo in California, leaving only five known northern square-lipped rhinoceroses remain on Earth.

▼ 關鍵字：

① 主詞：northern square-lipped rhinoceroses

② 動詞：leaving

在這篇文章中，從主題句可以掌握的是主詞北白犀和僅
剩五隻犀牛。

▼ 其他資訊：only five

only five 是補充説明主詞 northern square-lipped
rhinoceroses，全世界只剩下五隻白犀牛。

2. **抓末段重點** 了解第一段後快速掃描最後一段，因為最後
　一段是結尾，看完最後一段的主題句就可以
　粗略了解文章的走向。

↳ 主題句：

> Vitro fertilization (IVF) efforts are now undertaken to save the species from extinction.

抓頭

抓尾

▼ 關鍵字：save

　　文章末段提到保育員將運用試管受精，使白犀牛免於滅亡。

3. 抓各段的主題句：

↳ 主題句：

> 　　Not only because he was well beloved here at the park, but also because his death brings this wonderful species one step closer to <u>extinction</u>.

▼ 關鍵字：extinction

　　這一段是聖地牙哥野生動物園管理者的聲明，同樣能看出白犀牛正瀕臨絕種。

補強

 解析 ────────────────

01. **(B)**　Known 是 know 的過去分詞，在這裡的意思是「已知的」，後方還可以加 as、to、for，答案選 (B)。

02. **(A)**　**(A) 巨大的**、(B) 荒謬的、(C) 單調的、(D) 明顯的，犀牛的死對人們是巨大的損失，故應選 tremendous，答案選 (A)。

03. **(A)**　not only...but also... 表示「不僅……還……」，答案選 (A)。

04. **(C)**　在關係子句上，which 可以指前面的名詞，故應選 (C)。

05. **(B)**　(A) 當、**(B) 同時**、(C) 因此、(D) 最近，meanwhile 較符合語意，故答案選 (B)。

必學詞彙

> » **remain** v. 剩下；餘留；
> 繼續存在
>
> » **extinction**
> n. 滅絕；消滅
>
> » **endangered**
> adj. 瀕臨絕種的
>
> » **mate** v. 交配
>
> » **unsuccessful**
> adj. 不成功的；失敗的
>
> » **reproduce**
> v. 繁殖；生殖
>
> » **naturally**
> adv. 自然地；天然地

文法觀念

1. 44-year-old Angalifu, a male northern white rhinoceros, **died of** natural causes at the San Diego Zoo in California, leaving only five **known** northern **square-lipped** rhinoceroses, remain on Earth.

   - died of的意思是「因……死去」，後方接續名詞，表示死因，例：His aunt died of cancer 3 years ago. 他阿姨在三年前因癌症死去。

   - Known 是 know 的過去分詞，在這裡的意思是「已知的」，後方還可以加 as、to、for，例：My husband is known for his intelligence. 眾人皆知，我老公很有智慧。

   - Squared-lipped 屬於複合形容詞，複合形容詞有許多型態，此為形容詞—過去分詞的用法，例如：well-known 知名的、kind-hearted 心地善良的、well-educated 有素養的、middle-aged 中年的。

2. Meanwhile, preservationists at the Kenyan preserve also acknowledged that their one male and two female rhinos are incapable of reproducing naturally.

- Meanwhile 用來表示同一個時間點發生的兩件事,也就是「同時」的意思,例:I went on a date with my girlfriend. Meanwhile, my friend went to a concert. 我跟女朋友去約會,同時,我的朋友去看了演唱會。

 **中文翻譯**

瀕臨絕跡的白犀牛

四十四歲的公北白犀安加利夫,因為自然因素在加州的聖地牙哥動物園去世了,留下僅存的五隻北白犀在世上。

「安加利夫的死去對我們所有人來說都是一個巨大的損失,」聖地牙哥野生動物園管理者藍迪李哲斯在一項聲明中寫道:「不僅因為他在動物園中很受歡迎,也因為他的死讓該物種又往滅絕之路向前走了一步。」

嚴重瀕臨絕跡的北白犀中,其中一隻存活在加州,另一隻則住在捷克共和國動物園,而另外三隻則在肯亞保護區。目前,全世界只有一隻公犀牛,住在半野外的肯亞的佩杰塔動物保護區中。

聖地牙哥動物園先前企圖讓安加利夫與動物園中另一隻母北白犀諾拉配對,卻沒有成功。同時,肯亞保護區的保育員也坦承,他們的一隻公北白犀與兩隻母北白犀沒有辦法自然繁殖後代。現在必須靠試管受精的方法來使這個物種免於滅亡。

07

The Global Warming crisis

Annual global CO2 emissions growth has always been a major economic crisis. Yet, according to data from the International Energy Agency, for the first time in 40 years, annual CO2 emissions in 2014 __(1)__ at 32 gigatonnes, unchanged from the previous year.

Analysts said the slowdown in __(2)__ was attributed to changing patterns of energy use in China and in OECD countries.

Secretary of the Department of Energy and Climate ChangeEd Davey said the figures showed that green growth is achievable, "However, we cannot be complacent. We need to dramatically cut emissions, not just stop their growth," he added.

Countries around the world are aiming to get a new international climate change agreement at the United Nations Climate Change Conference, which was held in Paris __(3)__ December 2015.

To avoid "dangerous" climate change, more efforts should be made to limit the increase of the average global surface temperature to __(4)__ 2°C (3.6°F) __(5)__ pre-industrial levels.

___ 01. (A) was remaining   (B) had remained   (C) remain
        (D) ramained

___ 02. (A) missions   (B) emigrants   (C) emissions   (D) emissaries

___ 03. (A) at　　(B) on　　(C) in　　(D) of

___ 04. (A) no less than　　(B) no more than　　(C) much more than
(D) over

___ 05. (A) compared with　　(B) dealt with　　(C) completed with
(D) composed of

 解題技巧 ────────────────

抓頭

1. **抓主題句** 掌握主題句最快的方式就是抓主詞跟動詞，可以
很粗略的知道這篇文章的方向為何。

↳ 主題句：

> Annual CO2 emissions growth in 2014 has remained at 32
> gigatonnes, unchanged from the previous year.

▼ 關鍵字：

① 主詞：Annual CO2 emissions growth

② 動詞：remalned, unchanged

在這篇文章中，從主題句可以掌握的是全球二氧化碳排
放量和維持不變。

▼ 其他資訊：

32 gigatonnes 是補充説明主詞 Annual CO2 emissions
growth 排放量為 320 億噸。

抓尾

2. **抓末段重點** 了解第一段後快速掃描最後一段，因為最後
一段是結尾，看完最後一段的主題句就可以
粗略了解文章的走向。

↳ 主題句：

> To avoid "dangerous" climate change, more efforts should be made to <u>limit</u> the increase of the average global surface temperature to no more than 2°C (3.6°F) compared with pre-industrial levels.

▼ 關鍵字：limit

文章末段提到限制地表平均溫度的增長。

3. 抓各段的主題句：

↳ 主題句：

> Secretary of the Department of Energy and Climate Change Ed Davey said the figures showed that green growth is achievable, "However we cannot be complacent. We need to dramatically <u>cut</u> emissions, not just stop their growth,"he added.

▼ 關鍵字 ：cut

這一段是引述英國能源及氣候變遷部部長 Ed Davey 說的話，能看到他強調我們必須大幅減少碳排放量，而非僅是停止它們成長。

解析

01. **(D)** 由於二氧化碳是過去的事件，所以要用過去式，故答案應選 (D)。

02. **(C)** (A) 任務、(B) 移民、**(C) 排放**、(D) 使者，C 較符合文意，故答案應選 (C)。

03. **(C)** in 為介系詞，後方接月份，答案選 (C)。

04. **(B)** No more than 是「最多；不多於」的意思，文中氣候變遷大會希望地表平均溫度比過去升高不超過攝氏 2 度，答案選 (B)。

05. **(A)** **(A) 比較**、(B) 解決、(C) 連同、(D) 組成，文中氣候變遷大會希望地表平均溫度與過去比較，升高不超過攝氏 2 度，答案選 (A)。

 **必學詞彙**

> » **emission** n. 排放；散發
> » **crisis**
>   n. 危機；緊急關頭
> » **unchanged**
>   adj. 未改變的；無變化的
> » **slowdown** n. 減速
>
> » **attribute**
>   v. 把……歸因於
> » **achievable**
>   adj. 可達成的；可完成的
> » **complacent**
>   adj. 滿足的；自滿的

 文法觀念

1. Annual global CO2 emissions growth has always been a major economic crisis, but according to data from the International Energy Agency, for the first time in 40 years, annual CO2 emissions in 2014 remained at 32 gigatonnes, unchanged **from** the previous year.

 • From 是很常見的介系詞，意思是「從……」，例：I work from home. 我在家工作。（直譯：從家裡工作。）、I got a ring from my boyfriend. 我男朋友給了我一只戒指。

2. Secretary of the Department of Energy and Climate Change Ed Davey said the figures showed that green growth is achievable, "However, we cannot be complacent. We need to dramatically cut emissions, not just stop their growth," he added.

- Added 有轉述的作用，是「補充說明」的意思，既然是轉述他人說的話，代表已經是過去的事，所以動詞用過去式，例："I also bought you a gift" she added. 她說：「我還買了個禮物給你。」

3. To avoid "dangerous" climate change, more efforts should be made to limit the increase of the average global surface temperature to **no more than** 2°C (3.6°F) **compared with** pre-industrial levels.

- No more than 是「最多；不多於」的意思，例：She earns no more than 10 dollars an hour. 他一小時的工資不多於 10 美元。no more than 也可代表「只不過；僅有」的意思，意義上有些微的不同，例：He is no more than a nurse. 他只不過是個護士。

- Compare with 通常是「比較」的意思，例：Compared to British food, I prefer Taiwanese food. 跟英國菜相比，我偏好臺灣菜。這個用法容易和 compare to 混淆，compare to 還有「比喻」的意思，例：He compares women to flowers in his poems. 他在詩裡將女人比喻為花朵。

 **中文翻譯**

地球暖化的危機

　　每年全球二氧化碳排放量增長一直是重大的經濟危機,但國際能源署的資料顯示,四十年來第一次, 2014 年的全球二氧化碳的排放量,跟前一年一樣,維持在 320 億噸。

　　分析者認為排放量的減速,要歸因於中國及經濟合作發展組織(OECD)國家使用能源的形態改變。

　　英國能源及氣候變遷部部長 Ed Davey 說這數據顯示綠能成長是做得到的,「然而我們不能以此自滿。我們需要大幅地減少排放量,而非使排放量停止成長。」他補充。

　　世界各國正以能在 2015 年十二月於巴黎舉行的聯合國氣候變遷大會上取得新的國際氣候變遷協議為目標。

　　為了避免「危險的」氣候變遷,需要世人投注更多的努力,來維持地表平均溫度,希望和工業化時代之前相比,增加不要超過攝氏 2 度(華氏 3.6 度)。

08

The Additional Holiday

October 29, 2022

Dear Staff Colleagues:

I know that many of you are now beginning to make plans for the winter holidays. We all look ____ **(1)** ____ time with family and friends after a busy fall semester. ____ **(2)** ____ hard work is the foundation of TBS's excellence, we all need to balance work with time off for renewal.

Accordingly, I am pleased to announce that this year the company will give all staff both Friday, December 23, 2022, and Friday, December 30, 2022, as bonus days off, ____ **(3)** ____ the previously announced holidays on December 24 and 25 and January 1.

These bonus days will ____ **(4)** ____ all benefits-eligible TBS staff. The provision of necessary services will require some staff to work on December 23 and December 30. Supervisors will be in touch with those of you who need to come in those days, and will determine whether you can identify two other days to take as bonus days or will receive comparable pay. I ____ **(5)** ____ your flexibility and understanding.

I hope that these extra days off will make the upcoming holidays just a little bit more pleasant for each of you.

Best regards,

Maggie

Margarita S. Cliff

Personnel Manager

___ 01. (A) up　　(B) up and down　　(C) forward to　　(D) for

___ 02. (A) While　　(B) What　　(C) How　　(D) Which

___ 03. (A) according to　　(B) additionally　　(C) in addition to
　　　　(D) in order to

___ 04. (A) adapt to　　(B) adjust to　　(C) apply to　　(D) refer to

___ 05. (A) achieve　　(B) approach　　(C) abandon　　(D) appreciate

 解題技巧

1. **抓主題句** 掌握主題句最快的方式就是抓主詞跟動詞，可以
　　　　　　　很粗略的知道這篇文章的方向為何。

↳ **主題句：**

> 　　I am pleased to announce that this year <u>the company</u> will
> <u>give all staff</u> both Friday, December 23, 2022, and Friday,
> December 30, 2022, as bonus days off, in addition to the
> previously announced holidays on December 24 and 25 and
> January 1.

▼ **關鍵字：**

　　① 主詞：the company　　② 動詞：give all staff
　　在這篇文章中，從主題句可以掌握的是公司將給予員工
　　某個東西（某項福利）。

**抓
頭**

▼ 其他資訊：as bonus days off

as bonus days off 說明了公司要給員工的這項福利，也就是額外的假期。

2. **抓末段重點** 了解第一段後快速掃描最後一段，因為最後一段是結尾，看完最後一段的主題句就可以粗略了解文章的走向。

↳ 主題句：

> I hope that these <u>extra days off</u> will make the upcoming holidays just a little bit more pleasant for each of you.

▼ 關鍵字 extra days off

文章末段再次提到額外的假期。

3. **抓各段的主題句**：

↳ 主題句：

> These bonus days will apply to all <u>benefits-eligible</u> TBS staff.

▼ 關鍵字：benefits-eligible

這一段在講額外假期適用於所有符合福利資格的員工，同樣能看出郵件主旨跟假期有關。

 解析

01. **(C)** (A) 仰視、(B) 上下打量、**(C) 期待**、(D) 尋找，根據文章大家都期待著與家人朋友相處的時間，使用片語 "look forward to" 來表達，答案選 (C)。

02. **(A)** while 為連接詞，連接兩連續動作，故答案為 (A)。

03. **(C)** (A) 根據、(B) 另外、**(C) 此外**、(D) 為了要,只有 inaddition to 符合文意,故答案選 (C)。

04. **(C)** (A) 適應於、(B) 調整、**(C) 適用於**、(D) 提及,文中休假日將適用於所有符合福利資格的 TBS 同仁,故應選 apply to,答案選 (C)。

05. **(D)** (A) 達成、(B) 途徑、(C) 放棄、**(D) 感謝**,文中感謝員工的配合與體諒,故應選 appriciate,答案選 (D)。

 **必學詞彙**

» **renewal** n. 恢復;復原;復活;重建

» **previously** adv. 事先;以前

» **announce** v. 宣布;發布

» **eligible** adj. 合適的;合意的

» **necessary** adj. 必要的;必需的

» **determine** v. 決定

» **flexibility** n. 適應性;彈性;靈活性

 文法觀念

1. We all **look forward to** time with family and friends after a busy fall semester.

• Look forward to 是個常見的片語動詞,後方接名詞或是動名詞,例如:I look forward to Halloween. 我期待萬聖節,或 I look forward to hearing from you. 我期待您的回覆(這句經常用在商務往來的書信中)。

2. **in addition to** the previously announced holidays on December 24, 25 and January 1.

- In addition to 後方也是接名詞或是動名詞，例：In addition to the purple mug, I also got a pink one. 除了紫色的馬克杯，我還買了粉紅色的。

3. Supervisors will be in touch with those of you who need to come in those days, and will determine whether you can identify two other days to take **as** bonus days or will receive comparable pay.

- As 有許多不同的意義，在本句中，as 是「當作」的意思，例：I've always considered my cousin as my best friend. 我向來把表妹當作我最要好的朋友。

中文翻譯

額外的假期

2022 年十月二十九日

親愛的工作同仁：

　　我知道你們很多人都已經開始規劃冬季的假期。過了一個忙碌的秋季，大家都期待著與家人朋友相處的時間。雖然辛勤的工作是 TBS 繁榮的基礎，大家仍須在工作與休閒之間取得平衡才能繼續下去。

　　因此，我很高興地在此宣布公司今年除了原有的假日十二月二十四日，二十五日，以及一月一日之外，將讓全體員工再多休兩個禮拜五，包括十二月二十三日以及十二月三十日。

　　這多出來的休假日將適用於所有符合福利資格的 TBS 同仁。部分擔任必要差勤的員工仍須在十二月二十三日與三十日上班。主管們將會與這兩天需要來上班的同仁們聯繫，視情況決定是否要另外挑兩天休假或者直接領取相當的薪酬。感謝大家的配合與體諒。

　　希望這額外的休假能讓大家為即將到來的假日多增添一點樂趣。

此致，

瑪姬

Margarita S. Cliff

人事經理

09

A Baby of Miracle

36-year-old Allison Noyce went to the doctor ___**(1)**___ stomachaches when she found a lump in her stomach. She was afraid that she had cancer, but instead, medics told her she was pregnant. Just 12 days later, she gave birth to her daughter Sophie ___**(2)**___ weighed 6lb 4oz.

Allison Noyce was diagnosed with early menopause at age 20 and was told that she could never have children naturally. So when she and her husband Richard learned that she was ___**(3)**___ pregnant, but also very close to delivery, they were both astonished. "When a midwife arrived to discuss birthing arrangements, I thought I was dreaming," said Allison.

Allison said that her periods stopped completely when she was 20. "Since I've been with Richard I've never had a period. We'd already given up all thoughts of having a baby. We'd never used contraception."

Even doctors have no idea why Allison suddenly conceived after ___**(4)**___ through the menopause so many years.

"We are just enjoying our precious daughter–she is the ___**(5)**___ baby we never thought we'd have. We look at her and feel incredibly lucky," said Allison.

___ 01. (A) in (B) with (C) at (D) of

___ 02. (A) , who (B) which (C) who (D) what

___ 03. (A) not only (B) not (C) a (D) not at all

___ 04. (A) go (B) going (C) gone (D) went

___ 05. (A) magic (B) misery (C) miracle (D) miserable

 解題技巧

抓頭

1. **抓主題句** 掌握主題句最快的方式就是抓主詞跟動詞，可以很粗略的知道這篇文章的方向為何。

↳ 主題句：

> 36-year-old <u>Allison Noyce</u> went to the doctor with stomachaches when she <u>found</u> a lump in her stomach.

▼ 關鍵字：

① 主詞：Allison Noyce ② 動詞：found

在這篇文章中，從主題句可以掌握的是艾莉森和找到腫瘤。

▼ 其他資訊：

36-year-old 是補充說明主詞 Allison Noyce 的年紀。

抓尾

2. **抓末段重點** 了解第一段後快速掃描最後一段，因為最後一段是結尾，看完最後一段的主題句就可以粗略了解文章的走向。

↳ 主題句：

> "We are just enjoying our <u>precious</u> daughter–she is the miracle baby we never thought we'd have. We look at her and feel incredibly lucky," said Allison.

▼ 關鍵字：precious

文章末段寫的是艾莉森認為寶寶很珍貴，簡直是個奇蹟。

3. **抓各段的主題句：**

↳ 主題句：

> Allison Noyce was diagnosed with early menopause at age 20 and was told that she could never have children naturally.

▼ 關鍵字：early menopause

這一段在講艾莉森 20 歲時診斷出早發性更年期，被告知無法自然生育，可以看出文章跟懷孕生子有關。

 解析

01. **(B)** 身體上的疼痛通常都用 with，故答案選 (B)。

02. **(A)** 在非限定關係子句上，who 修飾的先行詞為獨一無二的物品或人，非限定關係名詞通常會在 who 前面加 "，"，故應選 (A)。

03. **(A)** not only...but also... 表示「不僅……還……」，答案選 (A)。

04. **(B)** 當兩個句子「主詞相同」時，為精簡句子並變化句型就可使用「分詞構句」。且依文意應用強調主動進行的 V-ing 分詞構句，應選 going，答案為 (B)。

05. **(C)** (A) 魔幻、(B) 苦難、**(C) 奇蹟**、(D) 悲慘，文中女孩是一個奇蹟寶寶，故應選 miracle，答案選 (C)。

 **必學詞彙**

> » **lump** n. 腫瘤；腫塊
> » **cancer**
>   n. 惡性腫瘤；癌症
> » **diagnose** v. 診斷
> » **period** n. 生理期
>
> » **contraception**
>   n. 避孕法
> » **conceive** v. 懷孕
> » **miracle**
>   n. 奇蹟；奇蹟般的人
>   （或物）

 文法觀念

1. She was afraid that she had cancer, but **instead**, medics told her she was pregnant. Just 12 days later, she gave birth to her daughter Sophie, who weighed 6lb 4oz.

   • Instead 在此作副詞，有「代替」的意思，後方必須加逗號，例：I told him to save the money he got from winning the lottery, but instead he spent it all on clothes. 我叫他把中樂透的錢存起來，但他反而把錢通通拿去買衣服。instead 也可作連接詞，後方加 of，例：I like to make my own bread instead of buying them. 我喜歡自己做麵包，而不是出去買。We'd **already** given up all thoughts of having a baby.

   • Already 指的是某個動作在過去已經發生，在句子中，後方要接過去分詞，或也可以放在句尾，例：I've already seen this film. 這部電影我看過了。

2. "We are just enjoying our precious daughter – she is the miracle baby we never thought we'd have. We look at her and feel incredibly lucky," said Allison.

- Never 屬於頻率副詞，在這裡表示過去從來沒有想過的事，所以動詞 thought 是過去式，never 是「從不」的意思，例：I neverliked eating meat. 我從來不喜歡吃肉。

 中文翻譯

奇蹟寶寶

三十六歲的艾莉森諾伊斯在發現腹部有腫瘤後，因為胃痛去看醫生。她擔心自己得了癌症，不過醫生卻告訴她，她已經懷孕了，而就在十二天後，她便生下了六磅四盎司（2380 公克）的女兒蘇菲。

艾莉森諾伊斯在二十歲時就被診斷出早發性更年期，並且被告知她絕不可能自然懷胎。所以當她和先生理查得知，她不僅懷孕，而且即將生產時，他們都震驚不已。「當助產士過來討論生產安排事項時，我以為我在做夢。」艾莉森說。

艾莉森說她的生理期在廿歲時便完全停止了。「自從我和理查在一起後，我就沒有過生理期。我們已經放棄所有生孩子的念頭。我們從不避孕。」

就連醫生也不知道為什麼艾莉森會在經歷更年期多年後，突然懷孕。

「我們真的好愛我們珍貴的女兒，她是個我們想都沒想過的奇蹟寶寶。我們看著她時，覺得自己真的是不可思議地幸運。」艾莉森說。

10

Miracle of Life

At age 12, Martin Pistorius fell inexplicably sick. He lost his voice and stopped eating at first. Slowly, he lost the ability to move by himself. Eventually, he fell into a coma. Doctors were unable to diagnose the exact ailment, but their best guess was cryptococcal meningitis and tuberculosis of the brain. They did not expect Pistorius to re-awaken or live longer than two years.

Yet, he didn't die. ___(1)___ , he started to regain consciousness and awareness at around 16. He was unable to impart this to the people around him, so ___(2)___ the next eight years, Martin was trapped in his body, with only his thoughts for company.

One day, an aromatherapist finally noticed that Martin, then 25, could ___(3)___ specific statements and questions she made. The Centre for Augmentative and Alternative Communication at the University of Pretoria later confirmed that Martin was aware.

___(4)___ took Pistorius 14 years to return to life. He began to communicate with others via a computer ___(5)___ with text-to-speech software, and now, he is a freelance web designer, a developer, as well as the author of the book Ghost Boy.

___ 01. (A) On other hand   (B) On the contrary   (C) Nevertheless
(D) Hence

___ 02. (A) for   (B) in   (C) at   (D) on

___ 03. (A) reach to   (B) rise to   (C) eject to   (D) react to

___ 04. (A) It   (B) It was   (C) This   (D) what

___ 05. (A) equipped   (B) agreed   (C) compared   (D) concerned

 解題技巧

抓頭

1. **抓主題句** 掌握主題句最快的方式就是抓主詞跟動詞，可以很粗略的知道這篇文章的方向為何。

↳ 主題句：

> At age 12, <u>Martin Pistorius</u> <u>fell</u> inexplicably <u>sick</u>.

▼ 關鍵字：

① 主詞：Martin Pistorius   ② 動詞：fell sick
→ 在這篇文章中，從主題句可以掌握的是馬汀彼斯特瑞斯和生病。

▼ 其他資訊：

age 12 是補充說明主詞馬汀彼斯特瑞斯的年紀。

抓尾

2. **抓末段重點** 了解第一段後快速掃描最後一段，因為最後一段是結尾，看完最後一段的主題句就可以粗略了解文章的走向。

↳ 主題句：

> It took Pistorius 14 years to <u>return to life</u>.

▼ 關鍵字：return to life

文章末段提到馬汀彼斯特瑞斯花了 14 年重獲新生。

3. **抓各段的主題句**：

↳ 主題句：

> Yet, he didn't die.

▼ 關鍵字：didn't die

這一段在講馬汀彼斯特瑞斯復甦的過程，同樣能看出他雖陷入昏迷卻還活著。

 解析

01. **(B)**　(A) 另一方面、**(B) 相反地**、(C) 然而、(D) 因此，On the contrary 較符合文意，故答案選 (B)。

02. **(A)**　for 為介系詞，常接一段連續的時間，答案選 (A)。

03. **(D)**　(A) 達到、(B) 能夠應付、(C) 拒絕、**(D) 對……有反應**，文中這位男人對某些問題有反應，故應選 eact to，答案選 (D)。

04. **(A)**　以虛主詞 It 開頭的句子，「陳述事實或還沒做的事」後多用不定詞 to V，答案選 A。

05. **(A)**　**(A) 配備**、(B) 同意、(C) 比較、(D) 關注，文中彼斯特瑞斯的電腦配備有語言軟體，故應選 equiped，答案選 (A)。

 **必學詞彙**

> » **inexplicably**
>   adv. 無法説明地；難以理解地
>
> » **coma** n. 昏迷
>
> » **ailment**
>   n.（尤指輕微的）疾病
>
> » **consciousness** n. 有知覺；清醒
>
> » **react**
>   v. 做出反應；反應
>
> » **return**
>   v. 返回；恢復；回復
>
> » **communicate** v. 溝通

 文法觀念

1. At age 12, Martin Pistorius fell inexplicably sick. He lost his voice and stopped eating at first. Slowly, he lost the ability to move by himself. **Eventually**, he fell into a coma.

   • By 是介系詞，後方連接名詞有「藉由」的意思，若要説明方法，by 後面的動詞則要是動名詞（V-ing），例：I learned how to do makeup by watching YouTube. 我看 YouTube 影片學會化妝。

   • Eventually 屬於時間副詞，用來表達事件發生的時間，eventually 是「終於；終究；最終」的意思，例：Brian eventually went back to university to finish his studies. 布萊恩最終回到大學去完成他的學業。

2. **Yet**, he didn't die. **On the contrary**, he started to regain consciousnessand awareness around 16.

   • Yet 在此是「然而」的意思，用在問句和否定句，可視句型結構放在句中或句首，例：She tried everything she could, yet still failed miserably. 她盡了一切的努力，然而還是悲慘地失敗了。

- On the contrary 是一個帶有轉折語氣的用語，後方需要加逗號，它的意思是「相反地」，用來反駁前面說的那句話，例：I thought the exhibition would be boring; on the contrary, it was very interesting. 我以為展覽會很無聊，相反地，展覽卻很有趣。

 **中文翻譯**

生命奇蹟

十二歲時，馬汀彼斯特瑞斯生了怪病。他先是無法說話和進食，慢慢地他身體沒辦法動，最後，他就陷入昏迷了。醫生無法診斷出他究竟得了什麼病，只能猜測可能是隱球菌腦膜炎和腦結核病。他們不認為彼斯特瑞斯會再醒過來，或是活超過兩年。

但是，他卻沒有死。相反地，他在大約十六歲時開始重獲知覺和意識。他無法將這件事告訴他身邊的人，所以往後八年，馬汀被困在自己的身體裡面，只有自己的思維相伴。

有一天，一個芳香療法專家終於在馬汀廿五歲時，發現他會對特定的句子及她的問題有反應。比勒陀利亞大學的擴大性及替代性溝通中心稍後也證實馬汀已經有意識。

彼斯特瑞斯花了十四年的時間，終於重獲新生。他開始透過建有語言軟體的電腦與他人溝通，而現在，他不但是個自由網路設計者、開發者，同時也是《鬼男孩》一書的作者。

11

America's Lowest Unemployment Rate

WASHINGTON -- The unemployment rate in the United States was reported at a two-year low of 8.8 percent in March of 2011. From 1948 until 2010 the United States' Unemployment Rate averaged 5.70 percent reaching an historical high of 10.80 percent in November of 1982 and a record low of 2.50 percent in May of 1953.

"They are very consistent with the view that the recovery is gaining some momentum. So the economy continues to recover; it's very good news," said Hugh Johnson, chief investment officer at Hugh Johnson Advisors in Albany, New York. U.S. Non-farm payroll employment increased ____**(1)**____ 216,000 in March. Job gains occurred in professional and business services, health care, leisure and hospitality, and mining. Employment ____**(2)**____ manufacturing continued to trend up.

The private sector accounted for all the new jobs in March, ____**(3)**____ 230,000 positions after February's 240,000 increase. Government employment fell 14,000, ____**(4)**____ for a fifth straight month as local governments let go 15,000 workers.

Although rising energy prices are eroding consumer confidence, economists do not expect businesses to put the brakes on hiring just yet.

"Employment gains have been modest in recent months, so in that sense I think businesses that were initially very wary of taking on permanent full-time employees are feeling more confident now than some months ago," said Richard DeKaser, an economist Parthenon Group in Boston. "___**(5)**___ they are more willing to make those kinds of long-term commitments."

___ 01. (A) by   (B) at   (C) in   (D) on
___ 02. (A) under   (B) on   (C) of   (D) in
___ 03. (A) and it add   (B) and adding   (C) adding   (D) added
___ 04. (A) appearing   (B) declining   (C) increasing
         (D) disciplining
___ 05. (A) Result in   (B) As a result   (C) On the contrary
         (D) As a whole

 解題技巧

1. **抓主題句** 掌握主題句最快的方式就是抓主詞跟動詞,可以很粗略的知道這篇文章的方向為何。

↳主題句:

> The unemployment rate in the United States was reported at a two-year low of 8.8 percent in March of 2011.

▼關鍵字:

① 主詞:The unemployment rate in the United States
② 動詞:reported

在這篇文章中,從主題句可以掌握的是美國的失業率和報導。

抓
頭

▼ **其他資訊**：a two-year low of 8.8 percent

a two-year low of 8.8 percent 是補充說明主詞失業率，創下兩年來的新低，百分之 8.8。

2. **抓末段重點** 了解第一段後快速掃描最後一段，因為最後一段是結尾，看完最後一段的主題句就可以粗略了解文章的走向。

↳ 主題句：

> Employment gains have been modest in recent months

▼ **關鍵字**：Employment gains

文章末段提到就業率逐漸升高。

3. 抓各段的主題句：

↳ 主題句：

> So the economy continues to recover, it's very good news.

▼ **關鍵字**：**recover**

這一段在講經濟持續復甦，能看出經濟在正面成長。

解析 ——————————————

01. **(A)** By 是介系詞，在此用來表達數量，答案應選 (A)。

02. **(D)** In 是介系詞，通常用來表達位置或方向，在此處，in 用來表達在某個產業，故答案應選 (D)。

03. **(C)** 當兩個句子「主詞相同」時，為精簡句子並變化句型就可使用「分詞構句」。且依文意應用強調主動進行的 V-ing 分詞構句，而對等連接詞通常會省略，故應選 adding，答案選 (C)。

04. **(B)** (A) 出現、**(B) 下降**、(C) 上升、(D) 管教，根據文章，政府減少提供一萬四千個工作機會，所以這五個月工作機會在遞減，故應選 declining，答案選 (B)。

05. **(B)** (A) 導致、**(B) 結果**、(C) 相反地、(D) 大致上，只有 as a result 符合文意，故應選 (B)。

 **必學詞彙**

» **average**
v. 算出……平均數

» **consistent**
adj. 與……一致的；符合的

» **investment**
n. 投資；投入

» **manufacturing**
n. 製造業

» **permanent**
adj. 永久的；長期的

» **economist** n. 經濟學者

» **leisure** adj. 休閒的

 **文法觀念**

1. Employment **in** manufacturing continued to trend up.

   - In 是介系詞，通常用來表達位置或方向，在此處，in 用來表達在某個產業，也是很常見的用法，例：Sandra is a photographer in the fashion industry. 珊卓拉是時尚產業的攝影師，或 In fashion, personality is the most important thing. 在時尚產業中，個性是最重要的。

2. U.S. Non-farm payroll employment increased **by** 216,000 in March.

   - By 是介系詞，在此用來表達數量，例：Water bills are expected to rise by 2% next month. 水費預計在下個月上漲百分之二。

3. Government employment fell 14,000, declining for a fifth **straight** month as local governments let go 15,000 workers.

   - Straight 有許多截然不同的意思，像是立刻、誠實的，而 straight 在此處則是「連續」的意思，例：We have been having junk food for three days straight. 我們已經連續吃了三天的垃圾食物。

美國失業率

華盛頓 – 最新發表的 2011 年三月美國失業率百分之 8.8，達兩年來新低。

從 1948 到 2010 年期間，美國平均失業率為百分之 5.7，1982 年十一月的百分之 10.8 為歷史高點，1953 年五月的百分之 2.5 為最低點。

「這與復甦逐漸出現動能的觀點非常吻合，因此經濟仍在持續復甦，這是非常好的消息。」位於紐約阿爾巴尼的休強森顧問公司的主任投資長，休強森這麼表示。

美國非農業就業人數在三月份增加了二十一萬六千人。專業與商業服務、健康看護、休閒、醫療與礦業的工作機會均增加。製造業的工作機會持續在成長。

三月份的新工作都來自於私人企業，繼二月所增加的二十四萬個工作機會，三月份又再增加了二十三萬個。政府提供的工作則少了一萬四千個，連續五個月遞減，地方政府也解雇了一萬五千名工人。

雖然能源價格的上漲侵蝕了消費者的信心，經濟學者並不認為企業會暫時停止招聘。「最近幾個月的就業正慢慢成長中，我認為比起幾個月前非常謹慎的心態，現在的企業已較有信心去接納長期工作的全職員工，」波士頓巴森農集團的經濟學家，理查德凱瑟如此表示，「因此他們較有意願去做這些長期的投資。」

12

The Advances in Medicine

In the world we live in today, rapid advances in technology seem to occur almost every day. New materials, computer simulations, and advanced ___(1)___ procedures mean that amazing leaps are made in almost every aspect of human life. From golf balls that go further to cell phones that are smaller and more powerful, we seem consumed with trying to create ever better products. There is one field where this quest for advancement does have real everyday human benefit. While we could argue backwards and forwards all day on the actual benefit of a smaller and more powerful cell phone, very few people would claim that advances in the medical fields are ___(2)___ beneficial. The advances we see in medicine are sometimes minor, like a better blood cholesterol tests, or robotic brain surgery. We are constantly finding new ways to diagnose illnesses, and treat them. Although many things cannot yet be cured, the treatments we have for them can be ___(3)___ advanced that the illness itself is ___(4)___ life threatening. Also, medicine, more than almost another field, is looking into the future. Today, scientists are working on projects that in 10 or 15 years' time may lead to even more astonishing advances. Genetic changes could result in infants having immunity from diseases at birth, in the possibility of patients been operated on by nano robots, and even in cloning human beings. Many ideas that only a generation ago seemed like wild science fictionare now actual research projects, with tangible results already being published. Technology has been the driving force behindmany of these advances. As we are more able to understand the processes behind illnesses, we are better able to remedy them with treatments. Computers have been a powerful tool in this process. They have allowed us to process more data __(5)__ could previously be processed in the lifetime of a researcher, in a day. As technology drives forward, so will its ability to help the doctors of tomorrow cure the epidemics of today.

___ 01. (A) manufacturing　(B) maintaining　(C) manifesting
　　　 (D) massacring
___ 02. (A) but　(B) nothing but　(C) anything but　(D) nothing
___ 03. (A) much　(B) so　(C) very　(D) such
___ 04. (A) no matter　(B) severe　(C) no longer　(D) ridiculous
___ 05. (A) , who　(B) , which　(C) which　(D) how

解題技巧

抓頭

1. **抓主題句** 掌握主題句最快的方式就是抓主詞跟動詞，可以很粗略的知道這篇文章的方向為何。

↳ 主題句：

> While we could argue backwards and forwards all day on the actual benefit of a smaller and more powerful cell phone, very few people would claim that <u>advances in the medical fields</u> are <u>anything but beneficial</u>.

▼ 關鍵字：

① 主詞：advances in the medical fields
② 動詞：are anything but beneficial
在這篇文章中，從主題句可以掌握的是醫學進步替人類帶來益處。

抓尾

2. **抓末段重點** 了解第一段後快速掃描最後一段，因為最後一段是結尾，看完最後一段的主題句就可以粗略了解文章的走向。

↳ 主題句：

> And as technology drives forward, so will its ability to help the doctors of tomorrow <u>cure</u> the epidemics of today.

▼ 關鍵字：cure

文章末段提到隨科技進步，能幫助我們在未來治癒流行病，可看出文章在說醫學和科技之間的關聯。

補
強

3. 抓各段的主題句：

↳ 主題句：

> Today, scientists are working on projects that in 10 or 15 years' time may lead to even more <u>astonishing advances</u>.

▼ 關鍵字：astonishing advances

這在講科學家的研究能帶來更大的進步，同樣能看出文章在討論科技進步。

解析

01. **(A)**　**(A) 生產**、(B) 維持、(C) 顯示、(D) 屠殺，文中先進的生產過程全都意味著人類生活中每一個領域的驚人躍進，故應選 manufacturing，答案為 (A)。

02. **(C)**　Anything but 的意思是「絕對不是」，答案選 (C)。

03. **(B)**　So...that...：如此以至於，答案選 (B)。

04. **(C)**　(A) 不管、(B) 嚴重、**(C) 不再**、(D) 可笑的，疾病的療法已經進步到疾病本身不會再對生命造成威脅了，故應選 no longer，答案選 (C)。

05. **(B)**　在非限定關係子句上，句首 which 可以指前面句子的所有資訊，非限定關係名詞通常會在 which 前面加 "，"，故應選 (B)。

Chapter 01 — 克漏字練習 —

069

必學詞彙

> » **simulations**
>   n. 模擬；模仿
> » **further**
>   adj. 更遠的；進一步的
> » **benefit** n. 利益；好處
> » **cholesterol** n. 膽固醇
>
> » **illness** n. 疾病
> » **epidemic**
>   n. 流行病；時疫
> » **technology**
>   n. 工藝；技術；科技

文法觀念

1. While we could argue backwards and forwards all day on the actual benefit of a smaller and more powerful cell phone, very few people would claim that advances in the medical fields are **anything but** beneficial.

   • Anything but 的意思是「絕對不是」，另外有個帶有相反意思的常見用法 nothing but「僅是」，經常容易搞混，例：He is nothing but a bully. 他只是個惡霸罷了。He is anything but nice. 他絕不是好人。

2. Genetic changes could **result in** infants having immunity from diseases at birth, in the possibility of patients been operated on by nano robots, and even in cloning human beings.

   • 可跟 result 配合的連接詞有很多，result in 後方接續的是結果，前方則要說明原因，例：Climate change could result in a disastrous outcome. 氣候變遷能帶來災難性的結果。

 **中文翻譯**

醫學的進展

在我們今日生活的世界，科技看來幾乎每天都在快速進步。新材質、電腦模擬器以及先進的生產過程，全都意味著人類生活中每一個領域的驚人躍進。從可以飛得更遠的高爾夫球到更小、功能更強大的手機，我們似乎一心想著要做出更好的產品。有一個領域的進步真的能造福人類的日常生活。當我們可能來來回回地爭論著較小的手機究竟有何好處時，很少人認為醫學方面的進步對人類沒有幫助。有時候，醫學的進步可以從一些微小（次要）的領域看出端倪，像是較好的血液膽固醇檢驗，或是自動的腦部手術。我們不斷尋找新的辦法來診斷及治療疾病。雖然很多疾病仍不能被治好，但是針對那些疾病的療法，已經進步到疾病本身不會再對生命造成威脅了。藥品不再只是醫學以外的分支項目，而展現出放眼未來的雄心。今日科學家們正在研究的項目，在未來 10 到 15 年後可能會有更令人驚訝的發展。基因變化也許會讓嬰兒在出生時，就對疾病有免疫力、讓奈米機器人有可能為病人動手術，甚至複製人類。在前一個世代許多想法，看來就像是天馬行空的科幻小說，如今已是實際的研究項目，而且已發表了實際結果。科技一直是這些進步背後的原動力。由於我們知道造成疾病的過程，所以能以各種療法加以妥善治療。而電腦便是這一過程中的強大工具。電腦讓我們能夠在一天之內處理完研究員可能要花一輩子才能處理完的資料。當科技進步，它也將能幫助未來的醫生治療今日的流行病。

13

Copyright

How we earn our living has changed drastically over time. A few hundred years ago, __(1)__ money, you needed to make something or help make something. From the farmer with his crops, to the manufacturer with his goods, whenever money changed hands, some goods or physical property did too. With the invention of the writing, this changed as now an idea could be written down and sold. However, if a person who sold the ideas came up with them by themselves, it is not too hard to imagine that they had some rights to those ideas. __(2)__ the rise of technology, more and more of what we use today is not a hard object in our hands, but rather an idea that someone turned into a program that we use. With so many people having so many ideas, there are always situations where two people claim to have both had the idea first. So much so that any software company today seems to employ more lawyers than people who code. The courts today seem full of endless trials between companies over a few hundred lines of ambiguous code that both parties claim belongs to them. As ideas get more abstract and technical, it becomes more difficult for a judge or jury to make a ruling on the validity of any one parties claims. __(3)__ a decision to be made purely on a point of law, the decision appears to be made more on which lawyer seemed to present themselves better, or whose expert witness was more able to explain the issues in a way that those making a verdict could understand them. Taken to the extreme, some privileged people now have the legitimate career of "expert witnesses." They go **(4)** , providing testimony on the issues as they see them, hoping to bias the judgment in the case towards **(5)** party is paying them for their appearance. How far we truly have come from the days when we had to make something to earn a living.

___ 01. (A) to make   (B) making   (C) we make   (D) for making

___ 02. (A) With   (B) On   (C) In   (D) At

___ 03. (A) Nothhing but   (B) Instead of   (C) No matter
     (D) Whether

___ 04. (A) case and case   (B) from time to time
     (C) from case to case   (D) time and time

___ 05. (A) that   (B) which   (C) however   (D) whichever

 解題技巧

1. **抓主題句** 掌握主題句最快的方式就是抓主詞跟動詞，可以很粗略的知道這篇文章的方向為何。

↳ 主題句：

> The invention of the writing changed as now an idea could be written down and sold.

▼ 關鍵字：

① 主詞：the invention of the writing
② 動詞：changed
在這篇文章中，從主題句可以掌握的是文字的發明和改變。

▼ 其他資訊：an idea could be written down and sold

an idea could be written down and sold 是補充説明文字的發明所帶來的改變。

2. **抓末段重點** 了解第一段後快速掃描最後一段，因為最後一段是結尾，看完最後一段的主題句就可以粗略了解文章的走向。

↳ 主題句：

> How far we truly have come from the days when we had to make something to earn a living.

▼ 關鍵字：How far we truly have come

文章末段提到我們不再像過去一樣必須生產物品去賺錢。

3. **抓各段的主題句**：

↳ 主題句：

> With the rise of technology, more and more of what we use today is not a hard object in our hands, but rather an idea that someone turned into a program that we use.

▼ 關鍵字：an idea

這在講我們現在不再使用實體物品，而是由點子而來的程式，同樣看到文章在比較過去和現代的生產方式。

解析

01. **(A)** to V 放置句首常用來表示「目的」，文中說人們為了達成賺錢目的 (to make money) 必須靠做東西，或是幫別人做事，故答案選 (A)。

02. **(A)** With 有許多不同用法，這裡用來表達「隨著」的意思，答案選 (A)。

03. **(B)** (A) 只是、**(B) 不但沒……反而……**、(C) 不管、(D) 是否，Instead of 較符合語意，答案選 (B)。

04. **(C)** From...to... 若後方接續相同的單字，通常代表「一個一個」的意思，有個常見的用語 from case to case 就是「一件一件地」，文中證人一個案子接著一個案子跑，故答案選 (C)。

05. **(D)** whichever 為複合關代，由 any+N 及 that 組成，故原句應為 hoping to bias the judgment in the case towards any party that is paying...，故答案 (D)。

 必學詞彙

» **drastically**
adv. 大大地；徹底地

» **manufacturer**
n. 製造商；廠商

» **abstract** n. 抽象概念

» **privileged**
adj. 享有特權的；特許的

» **ambiguous**
adj. 含糊不清的

» **judgment**
n. 審判；裁判；判決

» **appearance**
n. 出現；顯露；露面

 **文法觀念**

1. **With** the rise of technology, more and more of what we use today is not a hard object in our hands, but rather an idea that someone turned into a program that we use.

    - With 有許多不同用法，這裡用來表達「隨著」的意思，例：With the growth of the economy, the unemployment rate goes down year after year. 隨著經濟成長，失業率逐年下降。

2. They go **from case to case**, providing testimony on the issues as they see them, hoping to bias the judgment in the case towards whichever party is paying them for their appearance.

    - From...to... 若後方接續相同的單字，通常代表「一個一個」的意思，有個常見的用語 from time to time 就是「一次次地」，也就是「偶爾」的意思，例：His grandson visits him from time to time. 他的孫子偶爾會來拜訪他。

著作權

　　人們謀生的方式隨著時間徹底地改變了。幾百年前，你必須靠做東西，或是幫別人做事來賺錢。從農夫生產作物，到製造商生產物品，只要錢易手，物品或是物質財產也會跟著易手。隨著文字的發明，人的點子現在也可以寫下來出售。然而，如果一個人出售的點子是他們自己想出來的，那麼就不難了解他們對那些構想是有一些權利的。隨著科技的提升，今天我們使用的東西中，有越來越多是被人轉化為程式的點子，而非拿在手中的實體物品。而且因為很多人有點子，所以常常會有兩個人宣稱比對方更早產生某個點子。因為這種狀況太多了，每個軟體公司裡的律師人數，似乎都比電腦程式設計師來得多。今日的法院中充斥著沒完沒了的案件，就在審各公司堅稱它們有好幾百條，而且內容含糊不清的程式碼。當構思的點子越是抽象及具科技性，要法官或陪審團裁決當事人宣稱的合法性就越加困難。決定往往不是純粹出於法律觀點，而似乎是取決於哪一邊的律師辯護技巧更好，或是哪一邊的專家證人能讓陪審團理解問題的解釋。於是情況開始走向極端了。一些有特權的人現在以當專家證人為正當職業。他們一個案子接著一個案子跑，為爭議提供證詞，希望判決能偏向付錢請他們出席法院的那一方。從必須自己生產東西來討生活的日子，一直到現在，這中間真的歷經巨大的轉變。

14

The Key to Success

Have you ever watched a TV report on some new millionairewho has turned a speculative idea into a fortune? __(1)__ you would watch it and think, that is so easy and obvious and why didn't I think of it? Well, chances are, more than one person did come up with the same idea, and more than one person started up a company with the exact same idea. In fact, probably more than ten people did. So why is one on TV doing the interview and not the other nine? The answer is not luck, but good sense. While many of us have great ideas, few of us have the understanding of how a business really runs. The skills __(2)__ need people to invest in an idea and endorse it are not the same as those needed to bring a concept to manufacture, and to market. Too many businesses fail because smart people try to do all of these and other things __(3)__ the assumption that they can learn these skills. An exceptional few do, but for the vast majority get so tied up in trying to budget, build inventory, reduce risk and still expand to meet demand that almost invariably something gets missed. Currency fluctuations result in unexpected cash shortages, expensive manufacturers who don't meet deadlines and the hidden costs of borrowing can seem to skyrocket overnight. The best move most successful inventors and entrepreneurs make is to fire themselves. Instead of __(4)__ to be the CEO, President, CFO and CIO all in one, they realize that there are people out there with years of experience in these fields who presently surpass their skills in every way. An appropriate example is when the co-founders of Google effectively gave up __(5)__ to run their own company after 3 years, and hired a CEO. Having someone who understands there is more to running a business than just revenue has allowed the technical genius of the founders of Google to drive innovation after innovation, while the finance of Google has been left in capable hands and well taken care of.

___ 01. (A) No doubt   (B) No longer   (C) Nothing   (D) Never

___ 02. (A) when   (B) which   (C) what   (D) who

___ 03. (A) under   (B) in   (C) on   (D) of

___ 04. (A) try   (B) tried   (C) trying   (D) tries

___ 05. (A) try   (B) tried   (C) trying   (D) tries

 解題技巧

1. **抓主題句** 掌握主題句最快的方式就是抓主詞跟動詞,可以很粗略的知道這篇文章的方向為何。

   ↳ 主題句:

   > While many of us have great ideas, few of us have the understanding of how a business really runs.

   ▼ 關鍵字:

   ① 主詞:few of us
   ② 動詞:have the understanding of how a business really runs.

   在這篇文章中,從主題句可以掌握的是很少人真正了解商業運作的方式。

抓頭

▼ 其他資訊：

many of us have great ideas 補充説明有好點子的人很多。

2. **抓末段重點** 了解第一段後快速掃描最後一段，因為最後一段是結尾，看完最後一段的主題句就可以粗略了解文章的走向。

↳ 主題句：

> Having someone who understands there is more to running a business than just revenue.

▼ 關鍵字：there is more to running a business

文章末段提到必須有人了解做生意不只是要創造收益。

3. **抓各段的主題句：**

↳ 主題句：

> The best move most successful inventors and entrepreneurs make is to fire themselves.

▼ 關鍵字：fire themselves.

這在講多數最成功的發明家和企業家曾把自己解雇，同樣能看出文章在探討經營公司的要點。

 解析

01. **(A)**　No doubt 是「毫無疑問」的意思，只有 (A) 符合與意，答案選 (A)。

02. **(B)**　which 是關係代名詞替代先行詞 the skills，來引導**關係子句**，並修飾所替代的先行詞，答案應選 (B)。

03. **(A)**　Under 是「在……之下，受到……」的意思，答案選 (A)。

04. **(C)** of 為介系詞，後面接名詞，故應選動名詞 V-ing
"trying"，答案選 (C)。

05. **(C)** give up 後多接 V-ing，答案選 (C)。

 必學詞彙

> **speculative**
> **adj.** 思索的；純理論的

> **assumption**
> **n.** 假定；設想

> **exceptional**
> **adj.** 例外的；異常的

> **majority** **n.** 多數；過半數；大多數

> **inventory**
> **n.** 存貨；存貨清單

> **appropriate**
> **adj.** 適當的；洽當的

> **genius** **n.** 天才；天賦

 文法觀念

1. **Well**, chances are, more than one person did and more than one person started up a company with the exact same idea.

   • Well 的原意是「很好」，但常聽到用 well 來當語助詞或變成口頭禪，可以翻譯成「那麼」例：Well, then I think you should apologize to her. 那麼我想你該跟她道歉。

2. Too many businesses fail because smart people try to do all of these and other things **under** the assumption that they can learn these skills.

   • Under 在此的用法並不複雜，它是「在……之下，受到……」的意思，常聽到的 Driving under the influence (DUI)，直譯為「在（酒精）影響下駕駛」，也就是酒駕。

成功的關鍵

你曾經看過電視報導某個把投機的想法轉變成財富的新百萬富翁嗎？毫無疑問地，你看到後會想，這麼簡單又明顯的點子，為什麼我沒想到呢？嗯，有人想到點子，可能就有人會以同樣構想成立公司。事實上，可能會有超過十個人這麼做。那麼，為什麼上電視接受訪問的就是那一個人，而不是另外的九個人呢？答案不是靠運氣，而是靠良好的判斷力。雖然我們之中有許多人有很棒的點子，但是我們很少有人知道一個企業的運作方式。讓人們認同並投資一個構想所需的技能，與那些要將觀念用於製造和放到市場上銷售的技能，無法相提並論。很多企業之所以失敗，乃是因為自作聰明，以為自己能學會所有的技術。少數幾個人辦到了，但絕大多數的人忙著編預算、增加存貨、降低風險，以及擴大事業以滿足需求，然後總是忽略了某些事。貨幣波動造成意料之外的現金短缺、昂貴，不在期限內交貨的製造商以及借貸的隱性成本等問題，可能在一夜之間就會一口氣爆發。多數最成功的發明家和企業家所採取的最佳行動就是把自己解雇。他們非但不想擔任集團首席執行長、總裁、首席財務長和首席資訊長於一身的角色，反而理解到公司外面有些人才不但在該領域擁有多年經驗，而且現有的技術也都超越他們。一個適當的例子就是Google 的共同創辦人在三年後放棄經營自己的公司，而聘請了一位首席執行長。當 Google 的財務交到有能力的人手中，而且受到妥善的處理的同時，一個了解經營企業不僅是收益的人才，讓創辦 Google 的科技天才們得以推動一波又一波的改革。因為公司中有人了解到做生意不只是創造收益，創辦 Google 的那些科技天才才得以不斷地推陳出新，而同時 Google 的經濟狀況已經交給有能力的人，並且照顧得很好。

15

The Charm of London

London is the largest metropolis and main commercial centre in England. It is one of the largest and also one of the most cosmopolitan cities in the world. People from ___(1)___ have come to settle in London and brought with them a lot of different cultures. Being a shipping port situated on the River Thames, London is also one of the most important tourism destinations in Europe. Upon arrival at Heathrow airport, one of the busiest airports in the world, you will discover that an inexpensive and fast way to the city centre is via the Tube or the Underground system. This mode of transportation is often crowded, but very efficient. ___(2)___ you have a map of the underground system, it is not likely to ___(3)___ lost. Other world-famous modes of transport in London are cabs and buses.The London taxi, also called a cab, is always black. The red double-decker buses are especially unique to London. Buckingham Palace is the official home of the Queen. Viewing the changing of the guard there is fascinating. Other sightseeing sites include St Paul's cathedral, Westminster Abbey, the fountain in Trafalgar Square and the Tower of London. There are also plenty of museums and art galleries which are worth visiting. One thing you might complain about London is probably its climate. It rains a lot. It is often chilly, but is unlikely to get ___(4)___ extremely hot ___(4)___ extremely cold. In spite of its frequent rainy weather, London is home to two world-famous sporting facilities, both of which can only be used in good weather-Wimbledon Tennis Courts and Lords Cricket Ground. On sunny days, you can take a walk in the very beautiful Hyde Park or idle along the Serpentine River. London is a shopper's paradise. You can find expensive goods as well as budget bargains. Night clubs and live theatre shows make the night life exciting. __(5)__ the many exotic restaurants, there are also countless typical English pubs where you can enjoy the relaxing atmosphere while having a drink.

___ 01. (A) world around   (B) all over the world
      (C) over the world   (D) all through the world

___ 02. (A) As   (B) As long as   (C) No longer   (D) As soon as

___ 03. (A) got   (B) getting   (C) gets   (D) get

___ 04. (A) either;or   (B) neither;nor   (C) both;and
      (D) not only;but also

___ 05. (A) No more than   (B) Otherwise   (C) Other than
      (D) Perhaps

 解題技巧 —————————————————————

抓頭

1. **抓主題句** 掌握主題句最快的方式就是抓主詞跟動詞，可以很粗略的知道這篇文章的方向為何。

↳主題句：

> London is the largest metropolis and main commercial centre in England.

▼關鍵字：

① 主詞：London

抓頭

② 動詞：is the largest metropolis and main commercial centre

在這篇文章中，從主題句可以掌握到倫敦是首都以及主要商業中心。

▼ 其他資訊：

in England 是補充說明主詞 London 位於英國。

2. **抓末段重點** 了解第一段後快速掃描最後一段，因為最後一段是結尾，看完最後一段的主題句就可以粗略了解文章的走向。

抓尾

↳ 主題句：

> London is a shopper's paradise.

▼ 關鍵字：shopper

文章末段提到倫敦是購物天堂。

3. **抓各段的主題句：**

補強

↳ 主題句：

> One thing you might complain about London is probably its climate.

▼ 關鍵字：London

這在講倫敦的天氣，同樣能看出文章的主旨是倫敦。

解析

01. **(B)** 選項中只有 B 的意思是遍布全球，且也無另外三選項的用法，故答案選 (B)。

02. **(B)** As long as 的意思是「只要……」後方接上帶有主詞的句子，只要您有一張地鐵系統的地圖，就不太可能會迷路，故答案選 (B)。

03. **(D)**　be likely to 後要接原 V，故答案選 (D)。

04. **(A)**　**(A) 不是……就是……**、(B) 不是……也不是……、
(C) 兩者都……、(D) 不僅……還……，either;or 較
符合語意，故答案選 (A)。

05. **(C)**　(A) 不超過、(B) 否則、**(C) 除了……之外**、(D) 或
許，other than 較符合語意，故答案選 (C)。

 **必學詞彙**

> **metropolis**
> **n.** 大都市；首都
> **cosmopolitan**
> **adj.** 世界性的；國際性
> 的
> **crowded**
> **adj.** 擁擠的；擠滿人群
> 的

> **climate n.** 氣候
> **bargain**
> **n.** 買賣；交易；協議
> **frequent**
> **adj.** 時常發生的；頻繁
> 的
> **fascinate v.** 迷人；有
> 吸引力

 文法觀念

1. People from all **over** the world have come to settle in London
andbrought with them a lot of different cultures.

   • Over 在此是「遍布」的意思，要表達「全球」還可以說
   worldwide，例：This pop singer is an absolute worldwide
   phenomenon. 這位流行樂歌手澈底轟動全球。

2. **As long as** you have a map of the underground system, it is not
likely to get lost.

- As long as 的意思是「只要……」後方接上帶有主詞的句子，說明情況，例：I will take care of you as long as I am alive. 只要我活著，我就會照顧你。

 **中文翻譯**

倫敦的魅力

　　倫敦是英國的首都以及主要商業中心。它是世界上最大也最具國際性的都市之一。人們從世界各地帶著不同的文化來到倫敦定居。作為坐落在泰晤士河的港口，倫敦同時也是歐洲最重要的觀光地點。在抵達世界上最繁忙機場之一的希思羅機場後，你會發現一個到市中心便宜又快速的方法，就是搭乘地下鐵。這種交通運輸工具通常很擠，但非常有效率。只要您有一張地鐵系統的地圖，就不太可能會迷路。倫敦其他聞名世界的交通工具就是計程車和巴士。倫敦計程車都是黑色的，而紅色的雙層巴士更是倫敦特有的。白金漢宮是女王的宮邸。在那兒觀賞衛兵換崗是很令人著迷的經驗。其他旅遊地點包括聖保羅大教堂、西敏寺、特拉法加廣場噴泉和倫敦塔。那兒還有很多值得一遊的博物館和藝術畫廊。會讓你抱怨倫敦的，可能就是它的氣候。這兒常下雨。它通常是蠻冷的，但也不太會極熱或極冷。雖然這裡老是如此多雨，倫敦卻是兩大世界著名的運動場地一溫布頓網球場和上議院板球場的所在地，兩者都只能在天氣好時使用。在陽光明媚的日子，你可以在美麗的海德公園散步，或是沿著蛇形河閒逛。倫敦是購物者的天堂。你可以找到昂貴的商品，也可以找到便宜貨。夜店和實境劇場表演使夜生活充滿趣味。除了許多異國餐館之外，還有數不盡的典型英式酒吧，讓你可以在喝一杯的同時，一邊享受那輕鬆的氛圍。

16

Healthy Diet

Healthy diet is not just about paying attention to the nutrition labels, avoiding calories, or depriving yourself of the foods you love. Rather, it's about consumption of good nutrition, good meals that will make you feel energetic and keep yourself as healthy as possible–all which can be achieved __(1)__ learning some nutrition facts and incorporating them in a way that works for you. Choose the types of foods with ingredients that improve your health and energy levels and avoid the types of foods that elevate the risk for illnesses __(2)__ cancer, heart disease, and diabetes. One important principle is making sure to include a wide variety of food groups while planning your meal. An up-to-date healthy diet guideline is also helpful. What types of food are good for us? And what are those will jeopardize our health? In general, foods high __(3)__ complex carbohydrates, fiber, vitamins, protein, and minerals, low __(3)__ fat, and free of cholesterol are good. Such nutrition can be found in fruits, vegetables, grains, and legumes. A moderate intake of sugar and salt contented food is __(4)__ . Be aware that sugar, salt, trans fat and refined-grain products are often added to processed food products, so reading the nutrition labels before making a purchase will be a good idea. Fluid intake is also very important. Water, is an important element for healthy dieting as human bodies are about 75% water. It helps flush our systems, especially the kidneys and bladder. It definitely is a vital part of a healthy diet. The amount of food that we intake is also important, so make sure to keep portions moderate. Don't size __(5)__ the portion even if you think the food is in low calories. It is okay to treat yourself once in a while with those food that you are craving for as long as you watch the portion. Maintaining a balance between your calorie intake and calorie expenditure is the key. Healthy diet should also be accompanied with physical activities, so adding regular workout and exercise will make any healthy eating plan work even better.

___ 01. (A) by   (B) on   (C) from   (D) of

___ 02. (A) such   (B) as   (C) as for   (D) such as

___ 03. (A) by   (B) for   (C) on   (D) in

___ 04. (A) reconciled   (B) commended   (C) recommended
    (D) recognized

___ 05. (A) on   (B) up   (C) of   (D) from

 解題技巧

1. **抓主題句** 掌握主題句最快的方式就是抓主詞跟動詞，可以很粗略的知道這篇文章的方向為何。

↳ 主題句：

> Healthy diet is not just about paying attention to the nutrition labels, avoiding calories, or depriving yourself of the foods you love.

▼ 關鍵字：

① 主詞：Healthy diet   ② 動詞：is not just about
在這篇文章中，從主題句可以掌握的是健康飲食的重點。

抓
頭

抓頭

▼ 其他資訊：

paying attention to the nutrition labels, avoiding calories, or depriving yourself of the foods you love. 補充説明健康飲食不僅是注意營養成分標示、避免攝取熱量或是剝奪喜愛的食物。

抓尾

2. **抓末段重點** 了解第一段後快速掃描最後一段，因為最後一段是結尾，看完最後一段的主題句就可以粗略了解文章的走向。

↳主題句：

> Maintaining a <u>balance</u> between your calorie intake and calorie expenditure is the key.

▼ 關鍵字：balance

文章末段提到維持熱量消耗和攝取的平衡是很重要的。

補強

3. **抓各段的主題句**：

▼ 主題句：

> <u>Water</u>, is an important element for healthy dieting as human bodies are about 75% water.

▼ 關鍵字：Water

這在講水的重要性，同樣能看出文章的重點是健康飲食。

解析

01. **(A)** by 為介系詞，在此為「藉由」的意思，後面要接 V-ing 答案選 (A)。

02. **(D)** such as 為「例如」的意思，故文中有舉例食物中的營養成分時應用 such as，答案選 (D)。

03. **(D)** In 是介系詞，常用來講食物的營養成分，如同文章中的句子，答案選 (D)。

04. **(C)** (A) 不甘心、(B) 讚揚、**(C) 建議**、(D) 認可，文中作者建議應適度的攝取含糖和鹽的食物，故應選 recommended，答案選 (C)。

05. **(B)** Up 屬於介系詞，有向上或往上加的意思，除了像文章中的句子，用來說明食物分量之外，還能用來講衣服的尺寸，答案選 (B)。

 **必學詞彙**

» **deprive**
v. 剝奪；從……奪走

» **jeopardize**
v. 冒……危險；危及

» **ingredient**
n. （烹調的）原料

» **carbohydrate**
n. 碳水化合物；醣

» **principle**
n. 原則；原理

» **moderate**
adj. 適度的；有節制的

» **guideline n.** （常用複數型）指導方針

 **文法觀念**

1. Don't size up the portion even if you think the food is in low calories.

   • Up 屬於介系詞，有向上或往上加的意思，除了像文章中的句子，用來說明食物分量之外，還能用來講衣服的尺寸，例：I think you might need to go up a size. 我想你可能要穿大一號的。

2. In general, foods high **in** complex carbohydrates, fiber, vitamins, protein, and minerals, low **in** fat, and free of cholesterol are good.

   • In 是介系詞，常用來講食物的營養成分，如同文章中的句子，例：He has been eating a lot of food that are both high in fat and carbohydrates. No wonder he gained so much weight. 他最近常吃高脂肪、高澱粉的食物，難怪他胖了這麼多。

健康飲食

　　健康飲食不只是注意營養成分標示、避免熱量的攝取或是剝奪你對食物的喜愛。更正確的說，它是關於良好的營養攝取，好讓你精力充沛並盡可能保持健康的良好營養及餐點。這些都要靠學習一些營養的資訊，並將之納入一個對你行得通的方法中。以成分選擇食品的類型，可改善你的健康以及活力。要避免會提高如癌症、心臟病及糖尿病的疾病風險的食物類型。一個重要的原則是在規劃你的餐點時，一定要包括各種各樣的食物群。一個最新的健康飲食指導方針也是有幫助的。什麼樣的食物對我們好？什麼食物會危及我們的健康？一般來說，食物中含有高複合碳水化合物、纖維、維生素、蛋白質以及礦物質、低脂、零膽固醇是好的。這些營養素可以在水果、蔬菜、穀類、豆類中找到。建議適度的攝取含糖和鹽的食物。請注意糖、鹽、反式脂肪和精煉的穀類產品，通常被添加於加工食品中，所以在購買前閱讀營養成分標示會是個好方法。液體的攝入也很重要。水，是健康飲食中的重要成分，因為人體大約百分之七十五是水。它可以幫助清洗我們的系統，尤其是腎臟和膀胱。這絕對是健康飲食的一個重要部分。我們所攝取的分量也很重要，所以一定要吃適當的分量。即使你認為某種食物熱量很低，也不要多吃。只要注意食量，偶爾讓自己吃一次想吃的食物是可以的，關鍵是要保持熱量攝入和消耗的平衡。健康的飲食同時應伴隨著體能活動，所以增加規律的健身及運動，會讓任一種健康飲食計畫效果更佳。

17

Mutual Funds

For many years, the experts have argued backwards and forwards on where the best place to invest money is. Most people ___(1)___ agree that property was the safest bet; however, with the recent downturn of the world housing market, even that is uncertain. For most people, buying many houses is impractical. So they need to put their cash savings somewhere secure and earn some interest. Many agree that putting them in mutual funds is a safe option. A mutual fund is a collection of shares from different companies with diversification which is ___(2)___ by a commercial bank. You buy a portion of the fund, and the bank uses those funds to invest in a collection of stocks. Making the risk lower, they buy quotas of stocks from representative companies across the market, but the gains are not as great as they might be for a single stock. That's why many people like to target stocks directly. They can ___(3)___ make a lot more money if they have good luck. In some cases,a bit of background knowledge and research will result in smartdecision. However, too many people rely simply on luck, or a tip. Some people try various theories to project ___(4)___ might happen in the future, and buy accordingly. The stock market crash of late 2008 has proved that whatever research was done, much of investing in the stock market ___(5)___ luck, and sometimes that luck will be bad. Perhaps the best solution is to merge the two; The 60/30/10 rating is a good one. If you load 60% of your money in low risk mutual funds, 30 percent of your funds in low risk dividend paying stocks and gamble the rest like a Vegas roller, chances are you should at worst break even over time, and probably prosper well in the long run. Over the short term, you might be up 30% one week and down 40% the next. Yet, as long as you see sustainable growth in your portfolio, you have the correct strategy.

___ 01. (A) be used to   (B) used to   (C) use to   (D) using

___ 02. (A) administered   (B) admired   (C) admitted   (D) adapted

___ 03. (A) doubtfully   (B) dependably   (C) definitely
          (D) defensibly

___ 04. (A) where   (B) how   (C) which   (D) what

___ 05. (A) plans on   (B) depends on   (C) consists in   (D) insists on

 解題技巧 ─────────────

1. **抓主題句** 掌握主題句最快的方式就是抓主詞跟動詞，可以很粗略的知道這篇文章的方向為何。

↳ 主題句：

> For many years, the experts have argued backwards and forwards on where the best place to invest money is.

▼ 關鍵字：

① 主詞：the experts   ② 動詞：argued
在這篇文章中，從主題句可以掌握的是專家在爭論某事。

▼ 其他資訊：where the best place to invest money is.
由此看出，專家在爭論的是投資資金最好的地方。

抓
頭

2. **抓末段重點** 了解第一段後快速掃描最後一段，因為最後一段是結尾，看完最後一段的主題句就可以粗略了解文章的走向。

↳ 主題句：

> But as long as you see sustainable growth in your portfolio, you have the correct strategy.

▼ 關鍵字：strategy

文章末段提到投資策略，可見文章和投資有關。

3. **抓各段的主題句：**

↳ 主題句：

> Many agree that putting them in mutual funds is a safe option.

▼ 關鍵字：mutual funds

講將錢放在共同基金是安全的投資選擇，同樣能看出文章在討論理財投資。

 解析

01. **(B)** used to 用來表示過去經常做的行為，但現在不再發生了，過去大多數人會同意房地產是最安全的賭注，但現在卻不認為，答案選 (B)。

02. **(A)** **(A) 管理**、(B) 敬佩、(C) 承認、(D) 採用，文中說明共同基金是指一家管理大量不同公司股票的商業銀行，故應選 administer，答案選 (A)。

03. **(C)** (A) 疑惑地、(B) 可靠地、**(C) 絕對地**、(D) 防禦地，文中說明共同基金的投資客運氣好或絕對能賺到錢，答案選 (C)。

04. **(D)**　　what 為複合關代，由 the thing 和 which 組成，故
　　　　　　　原句應為 ...theories to project the thing which might
　　　　　　　happen...，答案選 (D)。

05. **(B)**　　(A) 計畫、**(B) 依賴**、(C) 堅持、(D) 堅持，文中
　　　　　　　說明股票市場的投資絕大多數還是靠運氣，應選
　　　　　　　depend on 答案選 (B)。

 **必學詞彙**

» **diversification**
　　n. 多樣化；經營多樣化

» **impractical**
　　adj. 不切實際的；無用的

» **various**
　　adj. 不同的；各種各樣的

» **sustainable** **adj.** 能保持的；能維持的

» **dividend**
　　n. 紅利；股票利息

» **accordingly**
　　adv. 照著；相應地

» **representative**
　　adj. 代表性的；代表的

文法觀念

1. The stock market crash of late 2008 has proved that whatever research was done, much of investing in the stock market **depends on** luck, and sometimes that luck will be bad. Perhaps the best solution is to merge the two; The 60/30/10 rating is a good one.

   - Depend on 是很常見的片語，除了本句中「根據」的意思，depend on 還有「依靠；仰賴」的意思，例：Her son is the only person she can depend on now. 她現在唯一能依靠的人只有兒子了。

2. Over the short term, you might be **up** 30% one week and **down** 40% the next.

   - 討論數據時，上升和下降是用 up 和 down 來表達，常見的說法有 go up / down by x%，例：Oil prices is expected to go up by 11% next week. 下星期，油價預計上漲 11%。

中文翻譯

共同資金

　　多年來，專家來回地爭論投資資金最好的地方是什麼。過去大多數人會同意房地產是最安全的賭注，然而由於最近世界房地產市場陷入低潮，即使是房地產也靠不住了。對大多數人來說，購買許多房子是不切實際的。因此，他們需要把現金儲蓄放在某個可以賺取一些利息的安全之地。許多人同意將錢放在共同基金是安全的選擇。共同基金是指一家商業銀行以多樣化的方式管理不同公司的大量股票。你購買一部分基金，然後銀行利用這些基金投資大量的股票。為了降低風險，他們會購買市場上具代表性的公司的配額股票，但獲利可能不會如單一股票那樣的好。這就是為什麼許多人喜歡直接以股票為目標。如果運氣好的話，他們絕對能賺更多的錢。在某些情況下，一點點背景知識和研究就能做出明智的決策。然而，太多人只靠運氣或是內部情報。有些人會用各種理論來推斷未來可能發生的事情，並根據推測來購買股票。2008 年年底，股票市場崩盤，已經證明了不管做了什麼研究，股票市場的投資絕大多數還是靠運氣，而且有時候運氣會很差。也許最好的解決辦法就是合併兩者，以 60/30/10 的比例來投資。如果你將你 60% 的資金放在低風險的共同基金、30% 的資金放在低風險的配息股票，並把剩下的拿來像賭城玩家那樣做股票投機，這段時間最壞的可能情況就是不賺不賠，但是從長遠來看可能為有不錯的獲利。在短期內，你的錢可能會一週增加 30%，並在下一週下降 40%，但是只要你的投資組合獲利能維持在一定水準，就表示你的策略是正確的。

18

The Importance of Credit Rating

While most people get wise to what a credit rating is and some even know their own scores, some people still know nothing about it and make common mistakes that affect their credit. To those who never borrow money, don't plan on ___**(1)**___ a house or a car on credit, their credit rating really is not that important to them. ___**(2)**___, most people will do at least one of these things in their lives, if not all three. Their credit rating will then make a contribution on whether or not a bank or other merchants will lend them money. A credit rating is a ranking of how likely you are to be able to reimburse a lender on time. Strangely it is not directly linked to how much money you make, but rather to how well you have managed your debt in the past. ___**(3)**___ unexpectedly, most people who have no debt have poor credit ratings. This is mostly because the banks have no history to go on as to whether that person would pay back debt if they had one. ___**(4)**___ get a good credit rating, here are a few tips. Firstly, you need to have a few credit cards which you constantly make more than a minimum contribution to. Having too many credit cards counts against your rating, as does any where payments are not consistent. Having interest payments on your credit card is not good, but missing overdue payments is much worse. One missed payment results in a lower score for ___**(5)**___ a couple years! Secondly, you should have some loan from a bank that is paid off on time and in full. A line of credit is an option, but a mortgage with a bank is much better. Last but not least, avoid bad debt. If you owe money and do not pay it off promptly or try to avoid it, the creditors can chase after you in court. If they do this, your credit history can fall very quickly, and will take years to prosper again.

___ 01. (A) purchases   (B) purchased   (C) purchasing   (D) purchase

___ 02. (A) On other hand   (B) Additionally   (C) However
      (D) Whatever

___ 03. (A) Somewhat   (B) Somehow   (C) Somewhere
      (D) Sometime

___ 04. (A) Due to   (B) In order to   (C) Owing to
      (D) In addition to

___ 05. (A) up to   (B) on   (C) under   (D) into

 解題技巧

1. **抓主題句** 掌握主題句最快的方式就是抓主詞跟動詞，可以很粗略的知道這篇文章的方向為何。

↳ 主題句：

> A <u>credit rating</u> <u>is</u> a ranking of how likely you are to be able to reimburse a lender on time.

▼ 關鍵字：

① 主詞：credit rating   ② 動詞：is
在這篇文章中，由主題句可得知文章主題是信用評價。

▼ 其他資訊：a ranking

a ranking 是用來解釋主詞 credit rating 的意義。

2. 抓末段重點 了解第一段後快速掃描最後一段，因為最後一段是結尾，看完最後一段的主題句就可以粗略了解文章的走向。

↳ 主題句：

> Last but not least, <u>avoid</u> bad debt.

▼ 關鍵字：avoid

文章末段提到要避免呆帳，同樣可看出文章在討論理財、信用方面的內容。

3. 抓各段的主題句：

↳ 主題句：

> In order to get a <u>good credit rating</u>, here are a few tips.

▼ 關鍵字：good credit rating

這裡寫的是得到良好信用評價的訣竅，同樣能看出文章主題。

抓尾

補強

 解析

01. **(C)** on 為介系詞後應接名詞，故應選動名詞 purchasing。

02. **(C)** (A) 另一方面、(B) 另外、**(C) 然而**、(D) 無論如何，文中在此句出現轉折，故應用 however，答案選 (C)。

03. **(A)** somewhat 用在不確定的狀況下，說不出確切原因的時候，可以解釋成「有一點」的意思，答案選 (A)。

04. **(B)** (A) 由於、**(B) 為了**、(C) 由於、(D) 此外，in order to 語意較通順，故答案選 (B)。

05. **(A)** up to 的意思為長達，文中說明，倘若欠債不還，會讓自己有壞的信用評價長達多年，答案選 (A)。

 必學詞彙

> **reimburse**
  v. 償還；歸還；補償

> **minimum**
  adj. 最少的；最低的

> **mortgage**
  v. 以……作擔保；抵押

> **mistake** **n.** 錯誤；過失

> **directly**
  adv. 直接地；坦率地

> **merchant**
  n. 商人；零售商

> **payment**
  n. 支付的款項（或實物）

文法觀念

1. **Somewhat** unexpectedly, most people who have no debt have poor credit ratings.

   • Somewhat 用在不確定的狀況下，說不出確切原因的時候，可以解釋成「有一點」的意思，例：Sarah was somewhat doubtful of John's explanation. 莎拉有點懷疑約翰的解釋。

2. If you owe money and do not pay it off promptly or try to avoid it, the creditors can chase **after** you in court.

   • After 在此作為介系詞，用來表示「在……之後」的行動，我們也常常看到 go after 這組片語，例：You should go after your dreams. 你該去追求夢想。

信用評價的重要

　　雖然大部分的人都知道何謂信用評價，有人甚至知道自己的分數，還是有些人對此一無所知，並犯下會影響其信用的常見錯誤。對那些從來不借錢、不計畫貸款買房子或汽車的人來說，他們的信用評價對他們真的沒那麼重要。然而，大多數人就算不是以上三件全都做，一輩子至少也會做其中一件。那麼他們的信用評價就會是銀行或是商人是否願意借錢給他們的考慮憑據。信用評價就是你是否能夠準時償還借款的評價。奇怪的是，這跟你賺多少錢沒有直接關係，而是跟你過去如何管理債務有關。有點出乎意料的是，那些大多數沒有負債的人的信用評價都很差。這主要是因為銀行無法從歷史紀錄中得知此人若是有債務的話，是否能夠償還所致。首先，你需要有一些你持續有做最低消費的信用卡。擁有太多信用卡，就跟沒有始終如一的支付欠款一樣不利於你的信用。信用卡使用循環利息是不好的，不過逾期未繳款更糟糕。一筆未繳的款項將會導致長達數年的低信用評價！其次，你應該有一些準時繳付並繳足的銀行貸款。信貸貸款是一種選擇，不過向銀行做抵押貸款會更好。最後還有一個重點是，避免呆帳。如果你欠錢又未準時還款或甚至試圖賴帳，債權人可以追你追到法院去。如果他們這麼做了，你的信用紀錄會掉得很快，而且要好幾年時間才有可能再恢復。

19

Personnel Management Policy

When you are employed by an enterprise or an organization,there is no denying that the personnel management policy of the company will influence you the most, from the first day you report in for duty to the day you resign or retire. In fact, the moment when you have your resume sent to the company, you are associated with the personnel of the company. First, your application will be screened and then you will be interviewed by the personnel director ____**(1)**____ is supposed to have an eye for placing individuals with the right skill sets in the right positions within the company. And once you are hired and enter the firm, you will be given an orientation at the beginning, followed by entry level training programs, and a series of continuing education programs designed for existing employees thereafter. The personnel management, which is sometimes referred to as human resources management, is the core of the entire company.

____**(2)**____ the things that have been mentioned above, the functions of the personnel management sector are also inclusive of drafting vacation, annual holiday, sick leave, maternity leave and absence for personal reason or absence for funeral policies, and healthcare program and insurances provided to the employees, such as health insurance and labor insurance. ____**(3)**____, it is also responsible for drafting operation policies and procedures, requirements for employment, commendation and disciplinary procedures, and even the dress regulations in the workplace. More and more employers or executive administrators of ___(4)___ understand that since employees are assets to their companies, a well-established personnel management policy is essential and indispensable. Besides various welfare policies, a well-schemed wage adjustment policy and a perfect career development strategy for promotion or transfer can also lower the turnover of staff and decrease the resignation rate. As for ___(5)___ educational programs, it is another way that the company invests in their employees in order to enhance their working skills and knowledge, which is beneficial not only for the employees but also for the company itself.

___ 01. (A) who   (B) that   (C) , which   (D) , who
___ 02. (A) Other than   (B) Otherwise   (C) Moreover   (D) Other
___ 03. (A) Whatever   (B) Moreover   (C) Over   (D) consequently
___ 04. (A) manufacturers   (B) factroys   (C) corporations
         (D) cooperations
___ 05. (A) continues   (B) continuing   (C) continue   (D) continued

解題技巧

1. **抓主題句** 掌握主題句最快的方式就是抓主詞跟動詞，可以很粗略的知道這篇文章的方向為何。

↳ 主題句：

> The personnel management, which is sometimes referred to as human resources management, is the core of the entire company.

▼ 關鍵字：

① 主詞：The personnel management

② 動詞：is the core of the entire company

在這篇文章中，從主題句可以掌握的是人事管理和公司的核心。

▼ 其他資訊：

referred to as human resources management 說明人事管理也稱為人力資源管理。

2. **抓末段重點** 了解第一段後快速掃描最後一段，因為最後一段是結尾，看完最後一段的主題句就可以粗略了解文章的走向。

↳ 主題句：

> More and more employers or executive administrators of corporations understand that since employees are assets to their companies, a well-established personnel management policy is essential and indispensable.

▼ 關鍵字：personnel management policy

文章末段提到越來越多企業雇主和主管了解人事管理制度的重要性。

抓頭

抓尾

3. 抓各段的主題句：

↳ **主題句：**

> Other than the things that have been mentioned above, the functions of the personnel management sector are also inclusive of drafting vacation, annual holiday, sick leave, maternity leave and absence for personal reason or absence for funeral policies, and healthcare program and insurances provided to the employees, such as health insurance and labor insurance.

▼ 關鍵字：the functions of the personnel management sector
這段在講人事管理部門的功能，同樣能看出文章主旨。

解析

01. **(D)** 在非限定關係子句上，who 先行詞為獨一無二的人；非限定關係名詞通常會在 which 前面加 "，"，故應選 (D)。

02. **(A)** **(A) 除了……之外**、(B) 否則、(C) 此外、(D) 其他，other than 語意較通順，答案選 (A)。

03. **(B)** (A) 無論如何、**(B) 此外**、(C) 超過、(D) 結果，Moreover 語意較通順，答案選 (B)。

04. **(C)** (A) 生產者、(B) 工廠、**(C) 公司**、(D) 合作，行政主管明白公司的人事管理制度是基本且不可或缺的，故應選 corporations，答案選 (C)。

05. **(B)** as for 為「至於」的意思，後面接 V-ing，答案應選 (B)。

 **必學詞彙**

> » **personnel**
>   **n.** 員工;人事部門
> » **individual**
>   **adj.** 個人的;個別的
> » **orientation**
>   **n.** 熟悉;適應
> » **requirement**
>   **n.** 必要條件;規定

> » **administrator**
>   **n.** 管理者;管理人
> » **essential**
>   **adj.** 必要的;基本的
> » **resignation**
>   **n.** 辭職;辭職書;辭呈

 文法觀念

1. First, your application will be screened and then you will be interviewed by the personnel director, who is supposed to **have an eye for** placing individuals with the right skill sets in the right positions within the company.

   • Have an eye for 是常見的用語,意思是「對於某事有獨到的眼光」,後方接名詞或句子說明,因此,後方擺動詞時,要加上 ing,例:Jeremy really has an eye for fashion design. 傑洛米真的對時尚設計有獨到的眼光。

2. Other than the things that have been mentioned **above**, the functions of the personnel management sector are also inclusive of drafting vacation, annual holiday, sick leave, maternity leave and absence for personal reason or absence for funeral policies, healthcare program and insurances provided to the employees such as health insurance and labor insurance.

- Above 的意思是「在……之上」，有一個常見的片語 above all, ...，意思是「最重要地……」例：Above all, the government must do anything within its power to protect the people. 最重要地，政府該盡一切所能來保護人民。

 中文翻譯

人事管理政策

　　當你受雇於一個企業或組織時，不可否認地，該公司的人事管理政策會影響你最鉅，從你第一天報到上班到你離職或退休那天為止。事實上，在你將履歷表寄給公司那一刻開始，就跟該公司的人事部門有關聯了。首先，人事主管會審查你的資格並面試你；人事經理應該要有能夠鑑別每個人的專業技能並將他安排在公司適當職位的眼光。而一旦你被錄取並進入公司後，公司一開始會幫你安排新人環境介紹，接著是新進員工的訓練課程，以及此後一連串為現有員工所設計的連續性學習課程。人事管理，有時也指人力資源管理，是一個公司的核心。除了上述事項之外，人事管理部門的功能還包括擬定休假、病假、事假、產假及喪假制度、保健方案以及提供給員工的保險，諸如健保及勞保。再者，它還要負責擬定營運政策和程序、雇用人員的必要條件、懲處及獎勵辦法，甚至是工作場所的服裝規定等等。越來越多企業的雇主或行政主管明白，既然員工是公司的資產，一個健全的人事管理制度是基本且不可或缺的。除了各項福利政策之外，規劃良好的調薪制度，以及完善的升遷或轉調等事業發展策略，也可以降低員工流動率以及減少員工離職率。至於連續性的教育課程，這是公司為了提升員工的工作技能和知識而對員工做投資的另一個方式，這不僅對員工有益，對公司本身也有好處。

20

Shifting Ice V.S. Environment

Barry Smit, a professor at the University of Guelph, has spent five years leading researches on how melting ice and changes in wildlife habits are ___(1)___ the livelihoods of far northern communities. He found that increasing difficulty in hunting for traditional food was leading to more junk food in the Inuit diet.

"The traditional diet is in fact very healthy for them," Smit said. "But because of the difficulties in hunting, people are___(2)___ their diets to what's available in the stores. The young people are increasingly eating highly processed junk food, so we are seeing more teeth and obesity problems."

The difficulties in hunting are caused by shifting ice and changing migratory patterns among animals such as seals, whales, and polar bears. Smit noted that the shifting ice made hunting and traveling more dangerous.

"The Inuit's respect for elders has been maintained by their wisdom about when and where to travel on the ice," said Smit. "But now elders will say it's safe to travel to somewhere at a certain time, but people still have accidents there. That ___(3)___ people's confidence in the traditional knowledge of the elders."

The United States' National Snow and Ice Data Center reported that the __(4)__ of Arctic sea ice cover at the end of November this year was the second lowest on record, and 12% below the 1979-2000 average for November.

"If you look over the next couple of decades, the transformation will be huge. It won't be an Arctic environment at all and people will have to __(5)__ their way of life completely," Smit said.

___ 01. (A) surprising　(B) exploring　(C) impacting
　　(D) developing

___ 02. (A) adapting　(B) according　(C) preventing　(D) admiring

___ 03. (A) approves　(B) defines　(C) undermines　(D) creates

___ 04. (A) environment　(B) massive　(C) extent　(D) population

___ 05. (A) understate　(B) modify　(C) understand　(D) preserve

 解題技巧 ─────────────────────

1. **抓主題句** 掌握主題句最快的方式就是抓主詞與動詞，可以很粗略的知道這篇文章的方向。

↳ 主題句：

> He found that increasing difficulty in hunting for traditional food was leading to more junk food in the Inuit diet.

▼ 關鍵字：

① 主詞：He (Barry Smit)　② 動詞：found

抓
頭

我們可以粗略得知，這是一篇關於某教授的研究與發現的文章。接下來要瞭解他的研究與什麼領域有關。

▼ 其他的資訊：

抓頭

difficulty in hunting for traditional food was leading to more junk food in the Inuit diet

說明這與因紐特人的飲食開始偏向垃圾食物有關，例如：

He spent five years leading researches on how melting ice and changes in wildlife habits 這裡提到溶冰與野生動物生態改變，也能作為判斷文意的線索。在接下來的章節裡，這些資訊將會被整合起來。

2. <u>抓末段重點</u> 瞭解第一段後快速掃描最後一段，因為最後一段是結尾，看完最後一段的主題句就能粗略瞭解文章的走向

↳ 主題句：

抓尾

> If you look over the next couple of decades, the <u>transformation</u> will be huge. It won't be an Arctic environment at all....

▼ 關鍵字：transformation

最後一段提到對「改變」的憂慮，跟第一段互相呼應。

3. **抓各段的主題句**：

↳ 主題句：

補強

> The <u>difficulties in hunting</u> are caused by <u>shifting ice</u> and changing migratory patterns among animals such as seals, whales, and polar bears.

▼ 關鍵字：difficulties in hunting/ shifting ice

這裡提到狩獵的難度與溶冰相關，換句話說，溶冰是間接造成飲食習慣改變的因素。

↳ 主題句：

> The Inuit's <u>respect for elders</u> has been maintained by their wisdom about <u>when and where to travel on the ice</u>.

▼ 關鍵字：respect for elders / when and where to travel on the ice

這裡提到對長者的尊敬與他們對溶冰的知識息息相關。

解析

01. **(C)**　(A) 令人驚奇、(B) 探索、**(C) 有重大衝擊或影響**、(D) 促進或發展，根據下一句提到飲食習慣改變的資訊，我們可以推斷這個動詞必定與「改變」相關，因此選 (C)。

02. **(A)**　**(A) 適應**、(B) 根據、(C) 防止、(D) 欣賞，Adapting to 是適應的意思，(C) 與 (D) 的後面不能加 to，而且字義也不符合句子要表達的意思，故選 (A)。

03. **(C)**　(A) 贊成、(B) 定義、**(C) 破壞、削弱信心**、(D) 創造，這裡提到的是老年人的生活知識遭到挑戰與否定，因此根據文意選 (C)。

04. **(C)**　(A) 環境、(B) 廣大的、**(C) 範圍**、(D) 人口，這裡提到的資訊與冰層面積有關，而 massive 是形容詞，在這裡詞性不合，故選 (C)。

05. **(B)**　(A) 輕描淡寫、**(B) 調整**、(C) 瞭解、(D) 保存，這裡主要提到的是生活方式的轉變，也呼應第一段的主旨，有著首尾相連的功用，因此按照文意選 (B)。

 **必學詞彙**

> **livelihood**
> **n.** 生活；生計

> **highly processed**
> **adj.** 經過特殊加工的

> **obesity** **n.** 肥胖；過胖

> **migratory**
> **adj.** 遷徙的；流浪的

> **community**
> **n.** 社區；共同社會

> **increasingly**
> **adv.** 漸增地；越來越多地

> **transformation**
> **n.** 變化；轉變；變形

 文法觀念

1. He found that increasing difficulty in hunting for traditional foodwas leading to more junk food in the Inuit diet.

   • Lead to 是導致的意思，後方接動詞或動名詞。
     例如：Reducing speed limits should lead to fewer deaths on the roads. 降低限速可以減少交通死亡人數。

2. But because of the difficulties in hunting, people are adapting their diets to what's available in the stores.

   • Adapt 如果後面加 to，代表適應不同情況而改變。
     例如：Many software companies have adapted popular programs to the new operating system. 許多軟體公司已改編常用的程式以適應新的作業系統。

3. The Inuit's respect for elders has been maintained by their wisdom

   • Respect 當動詞用後面加 for 代表對某人（事）的敬重。
     例如：I have great/the greatest respect for his ideas. 我非常尊重他的想法。

流冰 V.S. 生態

貴湖大學教授貝瑞・史密特花了五年時間,研究冰層溶解與生態改變對極北居民的重大影響。他發現狩獵傳統食物的難度增加,迫使因紐特人吃下更多垃圾食物。

「傳統飲食對他們的健康大有助益!」史密特說。「但因為狩獵困難,人們只好改吃商店販賣的食物。年輕人越來越常吃大量加工的垃圾食物,因此牙齒問題與過胖的問題也越來越多。」

海豹、鯨魚及北極熊等動物的遷徙途徑改變,加上流冰的影響,使狩獵變得困難。史密特注意到流冰讓狩獵與旅行變的更加危險。

「因紐特的長者知道何時何地走在冰上比較安全,他們的智慧維繫了族人對他們的敬意。」史密特說。「但現在,人們在長者指示的時間與地點外出,仍會發生意外,這使人們對年長者的傳統知識失去信心。」

根據聯合國國際冰雪資料中心的報告,今年十一月的北極冰層覆蓋比例,在歷年記錄排名倒數第二,而且比 1979 至 2000 年間的十一月平均數低了百分之十二。

「如果你觀察二十年後的變化,將會發現改變甚鉅。北極的原始環境將不復存在,人們的生活方式也必須徹底調整了。」史密特說。

Chapter 2.

閱讀
測驗

理解全文大意，再根據題議，
選出正確答案。

The Gift of Love

Will Pemble, a 50-year-old father of two sons, was asked if they could build a roller coaster in their own backyard after taking his family to an amusement park in San Francisco. "I thought about it for a second and the answer anyone expects is 'of course not'... but I said yes! I said sure!" Will Pemble recalled, "I couldn't think of a single good reason to say no."

After some consideration, the father took on the ambitious project to make his sons, dream come true. He headed off to the lumberyard for a few supplies and materials to build the ride, and threw himself into the gigantic DIY project.

Six months later, the committed father, with a little help from his 10-year-old boy Lyle, completed a nearly 200 feet long coaster in the backyard at their home in Orinda, California. This incredible homemade coaster is powered only by gravity and reaches a maximum speed of 14 mph.

Now Will and Lyle have started building a second coaster in a friend's backyard.

___ 01. Why did Will Pemble build a roller coaster?
 (A) He built a roller coaster for profit.
 (B) He built a roller coaster to impress his girlfriend.
 (C) He built a roller coaster for his wife.
 (D) He built a roller coaster for his sons.

___ 02. How long did it take for William Pemble to build this roller coaster?
(A) Six weeks.　(B) Six months.　(C) Six hours.
(D) Six minutes.

 解題技巧

1. **抓主題句** 掌握主題句最快的方式就是抓主詞跟動詞，可以很粗略的知道這篇文章的方向為何。

抓頭

↳ 主題句：

> Will Pemble, a 50-year-old father of two sons, was asked if they could build a roller coaster in their own backyard.

▼ 關鍵字：

① 主詞：Will Pemble　② 動詞：asked
在這篇文章中，從主題句可以掌握的是 Will Pemble 的兒子問他能不能蓋一座雲霄飛車。

▼ 其他資訊：50-year-old

50-year-old 補充說明主詞 Will Pemble 的年紀。

2. **抓末段重點** 了解第一段後快速掃描最後一段，因為最後一段是結尾，看完最後一段的主題句就可以粗略了解文章的走向。

抓尾

↳ 主題句：

> Now Will and Lyle have started building a second coaster in a friend's backyard.

▼ 關鍵字：second

文章末段提到 Will 和 Lyle 開始在朋友家的後院，搭蓋第二座雲霄飛車，可以得知他已經蓋了第一座雲霄飛車。

補
強

3. 抓各段的主題句：

↳ 主題句：

> After some consideration, the father took on the ambitious project to make his sons' <u>dream</u> come true.

▼ 關鍵字：dream

→ 這一段在講爸爸考慮過後，開始進行這項浩大的工程，能看出爸爸決定蓋一座雲霄飛車。

解析

01. **(D)** 第一題問的是 William Pemble 蓋雲霄飛車的原因，由第一段可看出兒子去遊樂園回來後，問爸爸是否能在後院蓋一座雲霄飛車，所以可以推得答案是 (D) He built a roller coaster for his sons.。

02. **(B)** 第二題問 William Pemble 花了多少時間蓋這座雲霄飛車，從倒數第二段 Six months later,... 能看出他花了六個月，所以可以推得答案是 (B) Six months.。

必學詞彙

» **roller coaster**
n. 雲霄飛車

» **amusement park**
n. 遊樂園

» **ambitious**
adj. 野心勃勃的

» **lumberyard** **n.** 木材堆置場；木料行

» **gigantic**
adj. 巨大的；龐大的

» **homemade**
adj. 自製的；像家裡做的

» **power**
v. 以……為動力

文法觀念

1. <u>Six months **later**, the committed father, **with** a little help from his</u>
   <u>10-year-old boy Lyle, completed a nearly 200 feet long coaster in</u>
   <u>the backyard at their home in Orinda, California.</u>

   - Later 為時間副詞，用來表示在某個時間點「之後」，反義
     詞 before 用來表示在某個時間點「之前」，例：I'll be back
     15 minutes later. 我 15 分鐘後回來。

   - With 是介系詞，是「跟……在一起；有」的意思，後方接
     名詞，例：She is going to Greece with her boyfriend
     tomorrow. 她明天要跟男朋友去希臘。The man is chasing
     someone with a gun in his hand. 那名男子手持一把槍在追人。

   - At 是介系詞，用來代表「位於某個定點」，表示確切的人
     事物或地點，例： That guy on the bus won't stop staring at
     me. 公車上那名男子不斷地盯著我。

2. <u>Will Pemble, a 50-year-old father **of** two sons, was asked if they</u>
   <u>could build a roller coaster in their own backyard after taking his</u>
   <u>family to an amusement park in San Francisco.</u>

   - Of 在文章中代表「所有格」，亦可用來形容「人」，人的
     性格、狀態或情況，例：It's rude of you to talk about his
     mom like that. 你這樣說他媽媽很失禮。

愛的禮物

　　威爾潘伯，一個有兩個兒子的五十歲父親，在帶家人到舊金山的一座遊樂園玩之後，孩子問是不是可以在自己家裡後院蓋一座雲霄飛車。「我想了一下，任何人都會以為答案是『當然不行』，但我說好！我說當然！」威爾潘伯回想道：「我想不到任何一個好理由來拒絕。」

　　在思考了一下之後，這個爸爸便接受這個讓他兒子夢想成真，野心勃勃的工程了。他前往木材場，尋找一些可以用來蓋雲霄飛車的用品和材料，接著便投入這個浩大的 DIY 工程。

　　六個月後，這個重承諾的父親，在他十歲兒子萊爾的小小協助下，完成了一座蓋在他們加州奧林達的家中後院，近 200 呎長的雲霄飛車。這座不可思議的自製雲霄飛車是以地心引力來提供動力，速度最高可以達到每小時 14 英里。

　　現在威爾和萊爾已經開始在一個朋友家的後院，搭蓋第二座雲霄飛車了。

The Cat that Came Back to Life

Zombie Cat Presumed Dead Found Alive after Burial

A cat thought to be dead was found alive after being buried for five days. The cat's owner Ellis Wayne Hutson said that Bart, the cat, was unresponsive after being hit by a car. Assuming the animal was dead, Hutson buried it with the help of a neighbor.

Yet, five days later, a different neighbor found the cat walking in her yard, presumably after he clawed his way out of the grave. The "Zombie Cat", covered in open wounds and dehydrated, was taken to the Humane Society for help. He not only underwent surgery to remove his left eye and have his jaw wired shut, but also had a blood transfusion.

According to court documents in Polk County, Florida's, Hutson was arrested and charged with cruelty to animals in 1998. The charges were later dismissed.

While Hutson wants his cat back, Tampa Humane Society is suspicious of the cat's home environment and the circumstances leading up to his burial; consequently, the director announced the group would not be returning the cat to its owner.

___ 01. What happened to this cat?

    (A) It died in a car accident.

    (B) It was buried alive after being assumed dead.

    (C) It became a ghost.

    (D) It went back to its owner.

___ 02. Why is the cat being referred to as a "zombie cat"?

    (A) Because it doesn't eat or drink.

    (B) Because it went through multiple surgeries.

    (C) Because it came back to life after being buried alive.

    (D) Because it constantly bites its owner.

 解題技巧 ────────────────

抓頭

1. **抓主題句** 掌握主題句最快的方式就是抓主詞跟動詞，可以很粗略的知道這篇文章的方向為何。

↳ 主題句：

> A cat thought to be dead was found alive after being buried for five days.

▼ 關鍵字：

① 主詞：cat　② 動詞：was found alive

→ 在這篇文章中，從主題句可以掌握的是，有人發現貓在被埋葬後的第五天死而復生。

▼ 其他資訊：thought to be dead

thought to be dead 是補充說明主詞 cat，主人原以為貓死了。

2. **抓末段重點** 了解第一段後快速掃描最後一段,因為最後
一段是結尾,看完最後一段的主題句就可以
粗略了解文章的走向。

抓
尾

↳ 主題句:

Consequently the director announced the group <u>would not</u>
<u>be returning</u> the cat to its owner.

▼ 關鍵字:would not be returning

文章末段提到動保協會會長宣布,將不會把貓歸還給主
人,可看出主人埋貓有可疑之處。

3. **抓各段的主題句**:

補
強

↳ 主題句:

Yet, five days later, a different neighbor found the cat
<u>walking</u> in her yard, presumably after he clawed his way out
of the grave.

▼ 關鍵字:walking

這一段在講鄰居發現貓在她家的後院走動,同樣能看出
貓在被埋葬後死而復生。

解析

01. **(B)** 第一題問的是貓的遭遇,由第一段的主題句可看
出主人將貓下葬,卻在五天後發現牠還活著,所
以可以推得答案是 (B) It was buried alive after being
assumed dead.。

02. **(C)** 第二題問貓被稱呼為「殭屍貓」的原因,從各段的
主題句看出這隻貓被埋葬後死而復生的情況,所以
可以推得答案是 (C) Because it came back to life after
being buried alive.。

必學詞彙

» **alive**
    adj. 活著的；現存的
» **bury** v. 埋葬；安葬
» **unresponsive**
    adj. 無答覆的；無反應
    的
» **grave** n. 墳墓；墓穴

» **wound**
    n. 創傷；傷口；傷疤
» **cruelty** n. 暴行；殘忍
» **suspicious**
    adj. 猜疑的；疑心的；
    懷疑的

文法觀念

1. <u>A cat thought to be dead was **found** alive after being buried for five days. The cat's owner Ellis Wayne Hutson said **that** Bart, the cat, was unresponsive after being hit by a car.</u>

    • Found 是「發現；覺得」的意思，後方接形容詞可以表達「發現；覺得」某人事物處於何種狀態，例：I found this movie boring. 我覺得這部電影很無聊。

    • That 是關係代名詞，可以用來代替 which、who、whom，that 前面不加逗號，例：My father ate the cake that I bought. 我爸吃了我買的蛋糕。

2. <u>**Assuming** the animal was dead, Hutson buried it with the help of a neighbor.</u>

    • 原句為 "Beacuse Huston assumed that the animal was dead,..." 前半句改為分詞構句，亦即「連接詞＋主詞＋動詞」"Beacuse he assumed..." 改為 V-ing（Assuming...）。

死而復生的貓

一隻被認為已經死了的貓，在被埋葬五天後又復活了。這隻貓的主人伊利斯韋恩哈特森說，巴特這隻貓在被車子撞了之後就沒有反應。因為認為貓已經死了，哈特森就在一個鄰居的幫助下，把貓埋了。

不過五天之後，另一個鄰居竟然發現這隻貓在她家院子裡走動，應該是從墳墓爬出來的。這隻全身都是開放性傷口，並且脫水的「殭屍貓」被帶到動物保護協會求助。牠不僅動手術移除左眼、用金屬線縫合下巴，而且還接受輸血。

根據佛羅里達州波爾克縣的法院資料，哈特森曾在 1998 年因為虐待動物被逮捕並被起訴。不過起訴後來被撤銷。

雖然哈特森想要把貓領回來，坦帕動物保護協會對這隻貓的居家環境，以及造成牠被埋葬的情況感到懷疑，因此協會會長宣布該團體將不會把貓歸還給主人。

03

Admission Notice

Dear Ms. Jennifer Bao,

It was a pleasure to meet with you last Friday, April 3, 2020.

We were very impressed with your outstanding book-editing background and your years at Caves Books. After discussing your application with our General Editor, I am delighted to offer you the position of editor-in-chief, with the salary of NT$42,000 per month. As for the benefits, you will receive National Health Insurance for you as well as labor insurance. More details will be discussed if you are interested in accepting the position.

Please give your serious consideration to this job offer and send me an acknowledgement by the end of this Friday, April 10.

We sincerely look forward to welcoming you to our team.

Best regards,

Andy Hsiao

Manager of Human Resource Division

___ 01. What can we learn about Jennifer Bao from this letter?
   (A) She has no related working experience in book-editing.
   (B) She just graduated from college this year.
   (C) She had a job interview last week.
   (D) She decided not to accept the job offer.

___ 02. Which job position was Jennifer Bao most likely to apply for?
   (A) The general editor.
   (B) The editor-in-chief.
   (C) The assistant editor.
   (D) The manager of human resource division.

___ 03. When should Jennifer Bao reply this letter at the latest?
   (A) April 3, 2020.
   (B) April 10, 2020.
   (C) The end of April.
   (D) The end of 2020.

 解題技巧

1. **抓主題句** 掌握主題句最快的方式就是抓主詞跟動詞,可以
   很粗略的知道這篇文章的方向為何。

↳ 主題句:

> After discussing your application with our General Editor, I am delighted to <u>offer</u> you the position of editor-in-chief, with the salary of NT$42,000 per month.

▼ 關鍵字:

① 主詞:I　② 動詞:offer
在這篇文章中,從主題句可以掌握的是寄件人和提供。

▼ 其他資訊:the position of editor-in-chief

the position of editor-in-chief 是補充説明寄件人所提出的
職位。

抓
頭

2. **抓末段重點** 了解第一段後快速掃描最後一段，因為最後一段是結尾，看完最後一段的主題句就可以粗略了解文章的走向。

↪ 主題句：

> We sincerely look forward to <u>welcoming you to our team</u>.

▼ 關鍵字：welcoming you to our team

文章末段說歡迎加入我們的團隊，代表這是工作邀約。

3. **抓各段的主題句**：

↪ 主題句：

> Please give your serious <u>consideration</u> to this job offer and send me an acknowledgement by the end of this Friday, April 10.

▼ 關鍵字：consideration

從這一段能看出出版社提出一件事，請鮑小姐考慮。

解析

01. **(C)** 第一題問的是鮑小姐做了什麼事，從郵件第一句可看出她上星期五參加了面試，所以答案是 (C) She had a job interview last week.。

02. **(B)** 第二題問鮑小姐應徵哪個職位，在第二段看到出版社提供主編的職位給她，所以答案是 (B) The editor-in-chief.。

03. **(B)** 第三題問鮑小姐最晚必須在何時回覆，在文章最後一段看到出版社請她要在四月八日前回覆，所以答案是 (B) April 8, 2020.。

 **必學詞彙**

> » **delighted** **adj.** 樂意的
> » **position** **n.** 恰當的位置
> » **consideration**
>   **n.** 考慮；需要考慮的事
> » **sincerely**
>   **adv.** 真誠地；誠懇地
>
> » **discuss**
>   **v.** 討論；商談；論述
> » **impress**
>   **v.** 給……極深的印象
> » **insurance**
>   **n.** 保險；保險契約

 文法觀念

1. After discussing your application with our General Editor, I am delighted to offer you the position **of** editor-in-chief, with the salary of NT$42,000 **per** month.

   - Of 是介系詞，加上 the position 來表示職位，應徵工作時很常用到，例如：I am writing to apply for the position of marketing assistant at your company. 我寫信來應徵貴公司行銷助理的職位。

   - Per 是介系詞，在此用來表示時間，是「每一；每……」的意思，例如：I spend 200 dollars on food per week. 我每個星期花 200 元吃飯。

2. **As for** the benefits, you will receive National Health Insurance for you as well as labor insurance.

   - As for 是介系詞，意思是「至於；關於」，例如：She will have a chocolate milkshake, as for me, a hot Cappuccino, please. 她要一杯巧克力奶昔，我則要一杯熱卡布奇諾，麻煩你。

中文翻譯

錄取通知

親愛的珍妮佛‧鮑小姐，

很高興在上週五2020年四月三日跟你會面。

我們對於你出色的書本編輯背景，以及在敦煌書局的資歷感到印象非常深刻。與我們總編討論過你的履歷之後，我很樂意提供你主編的職位，以及臺幣四萬兩千元的月薪。關於福利的部分，你將享有全民健保以及勞工保險。如果你對這個職位有興趣，我們可再來討論更多的細節。

請仔細考慮這個工作機會，然後在四月十日禮拜五前給我回覆。

我們誠摯期待歡迎你加入我們團隊。

此致，
Andy Hsiao
人力資源部經理

04

The Destructed Lake Nicaragua

Canal Could Turn Lake Nicaragua into a Dead Zone

The peaceful, rustic and splendid Lake Nicaragua is going to change dramatically with the pending completion of the $50 billion Nicaragua Grand Canal and Interoceanic Canal.

In 2013, Nicaraguan government granted HK Nicaragua Canal Development Investment Company (HKND) a 50-year concession to build and operate the 278-kilometer canal, which will create a huge new shipping route through Nicaragua by connecting the Atlantic and Pacific Oceans.

To carve a path for the canal, 30,000 people will have to be displaced. Not to mention the environmental impact on Lake Nicaragua. The wetlands may become more vulnerable to destruction and the damage to the quality of the water is nothing short of alarming.

"The ship traffic will pollute the water with toxic sediments and industrial chemicals and introduce destructive invasive species, plants and animals," said Dr. Jorge A. Huete-Perez, "Dredging of the lake for the construction of the canal will render the lake a'dead zone' because of hypoxia, eutrophication and turbidity."

___ 01. What's the main idea of this article?
   (A) There will be a new shipping route through Nicaragua connecting the Atlantic and Pacific Oceans.
   (B) The ship traffic along the canal will cause pollution.
   (C) The construction of the canal will turn Lake Nicaragua into a dead zone.
   (D) HKND was granted a concession to build the canal.

___ 02. What is the purpose of constructing the canal?
   (A) To preserve the environment.
   (B) To dispose toxic wastes.
   (C) To improve the quality of water.
   (D) To create a new shipping route.

 解題技巧 ───────────────────

抓頭

1. <u>抓主題句</u> 掌握主題句最快的方式就是抓主詞跟動詞，可以很粗略的知道這篇文章的方向為何。

   ↳ 主題句：

   > The peaceful, rustic and splendid <u>Lake Nicaragua</u> is going to <u>change</u> dramatically with the pending completion of the $50 billion Nicaragua Grand Canal and Interoceanic Canal.

   ▼ 關鍵字：

   ① 主詞：Lake Nicaragua　② 動詞：change
   在這篇文章中，從主題句可以掌握的是尼加拉瓜湖和它即將出現重大的轉變。

   ▼ 其他資訊：the pending completion

   The pending completion 是補充說明主詞 Lake Nicaragua 即將出現改變的原因。

2. **抓末段重點** 了解第一段後快速掃描最後一段，因為最後
一段是結尾，看完最後一段的主題句就可以
粗略了解文章的走向。

抓
尾

↳ 主題句：

> Dredging of the lake for the construction of the canal
> will render the lake a "<u>dead zone</u>" because of hypoxia,
> eutrophication; and turbidity.

▼ 關鍵字：dead zone

文章末段提到挖湖來建造運河會讓湖成為死域。

3. **抓各段的主題句：**

↳ 主題句：

補
強

> To carve a path for the canal, 30,000 people will have to
> be <u>displaced</u>. Not to mention the <u>environmental impact</u> on
> Lake Nicaragua.

▼ 關鍵字：displaced, environmental impact

這一段在講建造運河將導致三萬人被迫搬遷和環境問
題，同樣能看到運河對尼加拉瓜湖帶來的負面影響。

 解析

01. **(C)** 第一題問的是文章主旨，在這三個步驟之後可以得
知文章重點是尼加拉瓜湖將遭受汙染並成為死域，
所以只有 (C) The construction of the canal will turn
Lake Nicaragua into a dead zone. 最符合文章主旨。

02. **(D)** 第二題問建造運河的目的，從文章中可以看出目的
是為了創造新的運輸航道，所以可以推得答案是 (D)
To create a new shipping route.。

必學詞彙

» **rustic**
　adj. 鄉下的；質樸的

» **concession**
　n. 特許權；專利權

» **displace**
　v. 移開；迫使（人）
　離開

» **environmental** **adj.** 環境的

» **destruction**
　n. 破壞；毀滅；消滅

» **alarming**
　adj. 告急的；令人憂心
　的

» **destructive**
　adj. 毀滅性的；破壞的

文法觀念

1. In 2013, Nicaraguan government granted HK Nicaragua Canal
Development Investment Company (HKND) a **50-year** concession
to build and operate the 278-kilometer canal, which will create a
huge new shipping route through Nicaragua **by connecting** the
Atlantic and Pacific Oceans.

- 50-year 屬於複合形容詞，這是數字一單位的用法，例：28-
day，28 天的、8-mile，8 英里的、thousand-dollar，千元的。

2. "Dredging of the lake for the construction of the canal will render
the lake a 'dead zone' **because of** hypoxia, eutrophication; and
turbidity."

- Because of 是「因為……」，用來表示原因，後方接名詞，
例：Manny made friends with him because of his fame. 曼尼因
為他的名氣才跟他交朋友。

被破壞的尼加拉瓜湖

　　隨著造價五百億美元的尼加拉瓜大運河及跨洋運河的即將完工，原本平靜、質樸、壯觀的尼加拉瓜湖將產生巨大的變化。

　　2013 年時，尼加拉瓜政府准予 HKND 集團五十年的專利權，可以建造並營運這長達 278 公里，穿過尼加拉瓜，連繫大西洋與太平洋的巨大新運河航道。

　　為了鑿出一條運河的通道，有三萬人口必須被迫搬遷。更別提對尼加拉瓜湖所帶來的環境衝擊了。濕地可能會更容易受破壞，而且對水質的損害，簡直是令人擔憂。

　　「船運交通的有毒沉積物和工業用的化學製品，將會造成水污染，而且會引來毀滅性的侵略性物種、植物和動物，」佩雷斯博士表示，「為了造運河而挖湖，會因為組織缺氧、優養化和濁度而使湖成為一個『死域』。」

05

Erupting Island Rises from South of Tokyo

Erupting Island Rises South of Tokyo

While Japan is still in dispute with China and South Korea over uninhabited islets in the East China Sea and the Sea of Japan, it may get a freebie in the Pacific Ocean.

In November 2013, an underwater volcano erupted and its magma and lava have formed a small islet when molten lava cooled. The new landmass is about 500 meters off the coast of the deserted Nishinoshima island, about 1,000 kilometers south of Tokyo.

This islet has merged with its neighbor and continues to develop. Scientists said there is still plenty of magma to erupt and predicted the evolving islet would link up to the Nishinoshima island. In fact, the Japanese Coast Guard confirmed on December 26, 2013, that the two islands had joined up.

According to Japanese Coast Guard, owing to the volcanic eruption, Japanese island Nishinoshima has grown to 2.46 square kilometers, which is 11 times its original size and 52 times bigger than the Tokyo Dome. It is expected to get even larger because the volcano goes on erupting.

___ 01. What's the main idea of this article?
   (A) Japan, China and South Korea are in dispute over uninhabited islets.
   (B) Japanese island Nishinoshima has grown due to the volcanic eruption.
   (C) An underwater volcano erupted, and its magma and lava have formed a small islet.
   (D) Two islands joined up after the volcanic eruption.

___ 02. What is growing due to the volcanic eruption?
   (A) The islets in the East China Sea and the Sea of Japan.
   (B) The Tokyo Dome.
   (C) Nishinoshima island.
   (D) The territory of Japan.

 解題技巧

1. **抓主題句** 掌握主題句最快的方式就是抓主詞跟動詞,可以很粗略的知道這篇文章的方向為何。

↳ 主題句:

> In November 2013, an underwater volcano erupted and its magma and lava have <u>formed</u> a <u>small islet</u> when molten lava cooled.

▼ 關鍵字:

① 主詞:small islet　② 動詞:formed
在這篇文章中,從主題句可以掌握的是一座小島的生成。

▼ 其他資訊:magma and lava

magma and lava 是補充說明主詞 small islet 生成的來源。

抓頭

2. **抓末段重點** 了解第一段後快速掃描最後一段，因為最後一段是結尾，看完最後一段的主題句就可以粗略了解文章的走向。

↳ 主題句：

> It is expected to get even larger because the volcano goes on erupting.

▼ **關鍵字**：erupting

文章末段提到火山仍持續地噴發。

3. **抓各段的主題句**：

↳ 主題句：

> This islet has merged with its neighbor and continues to develop.

▼ **關鍵字**：develop

這一段在講火山噴發生成的小島和鄰近島嶼結合並持續成長、擴大，同樣可看出火山噴發與隨之生成的新陸地是文章重點。

抓尾

補強

 解析

01. **(C)** 第一題問的是文章主旨，經過閱讀的三個步驟和看過文章主題句 In November 2013, an underwater volcano erupted and its magma and lava have formed a small islet when molten lava cooled. 之後，可以得知文章重點是火山噴發與小島的生成，所以只有 (C) An underwater volcano erupted, and its magma and lava have formed a small islet. 最符合文章主旨。

02. **(C)** 第二題問火山噴發導致哪個地方生成、擴大，從文章中看出成長的是西之島，而非 (A) 東海、日本海的無人島、(B) 東京巨蛋、或 (D) 日本領土，所以可以答案是 (C) 西之島。

必學詞彙

» **dispute** n. 爭論；爭執

» **uninhabited** adj. 無人居住的

» **underwater** adj. 水中的；水面下的

» **erupt** v. 噴出；爆發

» **islet** n. 小島

» **merge** v. 合併

» **original** adj. 最初的；原本的

文法觀念

1. This islet has merged with its neighbor and continues to develop. Scientists said there is still **plenty of** magma to erupt and predicted the evolving islet would link up to the Nishinoshima island. In fact, the Japanese Coast Guard confirmed **on** December 26, 2013, that the two islands had joined up.

• Plenty of 是常見的片語，of 後方連接名詞，是「有許多……」的意思，of 不可以忽略，例：He has plenty of money, but he is not happy. 他很有錢，但他卻不開心。

- In fact 也是大家熟悉的片語，是「實際上；其實」的意思，能表達相同意思的還有其它說法，例如：actually、as a matter of fact 等。例句：They are not in love anymore; in fact, they broke up two weeks ago. 他們已不再相愛；事實上，他們兩週前分手了。

- On 是時間介系詞，用在星期幾、指定某一天，或是特定的日期，例：We visited Spain on February 14th, 1987. 我們在 1987 年 2 月 14 日造訪西班牙。

2. It is expected to get **even** larger because the volcano goes on erupting.

- Even 出現在句子中，經常有強調作用，是「甚至」的意思，例：Brandon has been in love with Molly for 5 years, but she doesn't even know who he is. 布蘭登暗戀莫莉五年了，但她甚至不知道他是誰。

東京南方海域升起的火山島

　　雖然日本與中國及南韓對東海及日本海上無人居住的島嶼之權利爭議尚未停歇，卻有可能不花分毫就得到太平洋上的一塊領土。

　　2013 年十一月，一個海底火山爆發，其岩漿和熔岩在熔岩冷卻後，已經形成了一座小島。這塊新的陸地離無人居住的西之島海岸約五百公尺，在東京以南約一千公里處。

　　這個小島合併了週邊臨島，而且還在持續擴大中。科學家認為還有很多的岩漿等著噴發，並且預測這個發展中的島嶼會跟西之島連起來。事實上，日本海上保安廳在 2013 年的十二月二十六日已經證實，兩座島已經接合起來了。

　　日本海上保安廳表示，由於火山爆發，日本西之島面積已經擴增至 2.46 平方公里，比原來大了 11 倍之多，而且比 52 個東京巨蛋還要大。因為火山還在持續噴發，因此這個島可預期會變得更大。

06

The Moon is Moving Further fram Earth

The Moon is Slowly Moving Away from Earth

The Moon is around 18 times further away from Earth than when it was formed 4.5 billion years ago. More precisely, the Moon is on the move with a speed of about 4 cm a year, which is as fast as our fingernails grow.

According to laser ranging measurements made since the 1970's using the Apollo "corner cube reflectors" deposited on the surface by the astronauts, the semi-major axis of the lunar orbit is increasing by 3.8 centimeters/year.

However, the Moon will never totally leave the Earth. Instead,Earth would eventually spin at the same rate that the Moon orbits. In consequence, Earth and Moon would be in equilibrium and the Moon would stop spiraling away.

It is expected that in 15 billion years, the orbit will stabilize at 1.6 times its present size, and the Earth day will be 55 days long equal to the time it will take the Moon to orbit the Earth. But long before that, the Sun will have expanded to become a red giant star, engulfed the Earth-Moon system, and incinerated it.

___ 01. What's the main idea of this article?
   (A) Astronauts had been using the Apollo "corner cube reflectors" to make measurements since the 1970's.
   (B) The Sun will become a red giant star.
   (C) The Earth-Moon system will be engulfed and incinerated by the Sun.
   (D) The moon is moving away from the Sun.

___ 02. According to the article, what is expected to happen in 15 billion years?
   (A) The Moon will totally leave the Earth.
   (B) The Moon orbit will stabilize.
   (C) The Moon will be around 18 times further away from Earth than now.
   (D) The lunar orbit will start increasing by 3.8 centimeters per year.

 解題技巧 ━━━━━━━━━━━━━━━━━━━━━━

1. **抓主題句** 掌握主題句最快的方式就是抓主詞跟動詞，可以很粗略的知道這篇文章的方向為何。

↳ 主題句：

> The Moon is around 18 times further away from Earth than when it was formed 4.5 billion years ago.

抓頭

▼ 關鍵字：

① 主詞：The Moon   ② 形容詞：further

在這篇文章中，從主題句可以掌握的是月亮和離地球更遠這件事。

▼ 其他資訊：

18 times 是補充說明月亮離地球更遠 18 倍。

2. **抓末段重點** 了解第一段後快速掃描最後一段，因為最後
一段是結尾，看完最後一段的主題句就可以
粗略了解文章的走向。

↳ 主題句：

> It is expected that in 15 billion years, the orbit will
> stabilize at 1.6 times its present size.

▼ 關鍵字：stabilize

文章末段提到運行軌道將固定下來，不再變動。

3. **抓各段的主題句**：

↳ 主題句：

> According to laser ranging measurements made since the
> 1970's using the Apollo "corner cube reflectors" deposited on
> the surface by the astronauts, the semi-major axis of the lunar
> orbit is increasing by 3.8 centimeters / year.

▼ 關鍵字：increasing

這一段在講月球運行軌道的半長軸每年持續增加，同樣
能看出月亮離地球越來越遠。

 解析

01. **(D)** 第一題問的是文章主旨，從文章第一段的主題句
The Moon is around 18 times further away from Earth
than when it was formed 4.5 billion years ago. 和各段
主軸可以看出來，文章重點是月亮離地球越來越
遠，所以只有 (D) The moon is moving away from the
Sun. 最符合文章主旨。

02. **(B)** 第二題問一百五十億年後會發生什麼事，從最後一段的主題句 It is expected that in 15 billion years, the orbit will stabilize at 1.6 times its present size. 可看出運行軌道會固定下來，所以答案是 (B) The Moon orbit will stabilize.。

 **必學詞彙**

» **lunar**
　　adj. 按月球的運轉測定的

» **spin** **v.** 旋轉；自旋

» **equilibrium**
　　n. 相稱；平衡

» **stabilize** **v.** 使穩定；使穩固

» **orbit**
　　v. （天體的）軌道運行

» **engulf** **v.** 吞噬；吞沒

» **incinerate**
　　v. 燒成灰；焚化

 文法觀念

1. The Moon is around 18 times further away from Earth than when it was formed 4.5 billion years **ago**. **More precisely**, the Moon is on the move with a speed of about 4 cm a year, which is **as fast as** our fingernails grow.

　• Ago 是「（時間）前」的意思，用法很單純，時間（多久以前）＋ ago，從說話時開始往前推算時間，例：I went to Thailand two weeks ago. 我兩週前去了泰國。

- → More precisely 為連接副詞，表示「更精確地説……」有重申的意味，例：The book is about French history; more precisely, it is about the French Revolution. 這本書寫的是法國歷史，更精確地説，這本書寫的是法國大革命。

- As fast as，as...as 是很常見的句型，用來表達「相等」的意思，後方多接形容詞，例：I love animals as much as you (do). 我跟你一樣愛動物。do 可寫出來，也可以省略。

2. <u>According to laser ranging measurements made **since** the 1970's using the Apollo "corner cube reflectors" deposited on the surface by the astronauts, the semi-major axis of the lunar orbit is increasing by 3.8 centimeters/year.</u>

- Since 在此代表「時間點」，since 也可以用來説明「原因」，例：Since she lives in China, she can't go on YouTube easily. 因為她住中國，她無法輕易瀏覽 YouTube 網站。

月亮離地球愈來愈遠

比起四十五億年前剛形成時，月球離地球的距離已經遠了 18 倍。更精確地說，月球是以每年約四公分的速度在遠離地球，就跟我們指甲生長的速度一樣快。

根據 1970 年阿波羅計劃時，太空人放在月球表面的「頂角反射稜鏡」的雷射測距法所測，月球運行軌道的半長軸以每年 3.8 公分的速度增加。

然而，月球永遠不會完全離開地球。相反地，地球最終會以跟月球運行一樣的速度自轉。因此，地球和月球會取得平衡，月球就會停止轉離。

一百五十億年後，運行軌道會在比目前大 1.6 倍之處固定下來，那時月球繞行地球一周的時間會是 55 天。但是早在那之前，太陽就已經擴大成一個紅色的巨型星球，吞噬掉地球—月球體系，並將之燒成灰燼。

07

Anophthalmia

When Kelly Lopez, who had a normal pregnancy, gave birth to a baby boy in Mesa, Arizona. She didn't think much of the fact that her baby wasn't opening his eyes while staff at Arizona's Banner Desert Medical Center initially thought the newborn's face was swollen.

The baby Richie Lopez had an MRI 13 days later, and the traumatic discovery was that his eyelids weren't open because he had no eyeballs beneath those closed lids — an extremely rare condition called Anophthalmia.

Lopez said, "The first thought through my mind was, how did this even happen and how was it not even caught?" Nevertheless, Kelly Lopez and her husband are still optimistic that science will progress enough to help Richie, who does have an optic nerve, see one day.

The three-month-old had surgery to be fitted with expanders in his sockets, so that they will grow enough to hold a prosthetic eyeball in the future.

___ 01. What's the main idea of this article?
  (A) Kelly Lopez gave birth to a baby boy.
  (B) The hospital thought the baby boy has a swollen face.
  (C) The baby boy went through a surgery at three months old.
  (D) The baby boy had an extremely rare condition called Anophthalmia, so he has no eyeballs.

___ 02. Why did the hospital fit expanders in Richie's sockets?
   (A) Because they wanted to help him develop his optic nerves.
   (B) Because they wanted to help his sockets grow big enough to
       hold prosthetic eyes.
   (C) Because they made a mistake.
   (D) Because his eyes won't open.

 ## 解題技巧

1. **抓主題句** 掌握主題句最快的方式就是抓主詞跟動詞,可以
   很粗略的知道這篇文章的方向為何。

   ↳ 主題句:

   > The baby Richie Lopez had an MRI 13 days later, and the
   > traumatic discovery was that his eyelids weren't open because
   > he had no eyeballs beneath those closed lids — an extremely
   > rare condition called Anophthalmia.

   ▼ 關鍵字:

   ① 主詞:Richie Lopez　② 動詞:had no eyeballs
   在這篇文章中,從主題句可以掌握的是 Richie Lopez 以
   及沒有眼球這件事。

   ▼ 其他資訊:

   The baby 是補充說明主詞 Richie Lopez 是小嬰兒。

抓
尾

2. **抓末段重點** 了解第一段後快速掃描最後一段，因為最後
一段是結尾，看完最後一段的主題句就可以
粗略了解文章的走向。

↳ 主題句：

> The three-month-old had surgery to be fitted with
> expanders in his sockets, so that they will grow enough to
> hold a prosthetic eyeball in the future.

▼ 關鍵 ：prosthetic eyeball

文章末段提到瑞奇動了手術，為了準備在未來裝義眼。

補
強

3. **抓各段的主題句**：

↳ 主題句：

> Nevertheless, Kelly Lopez and her husband are still
> optimistic that science will progress enough to help Richie,
> who does have an optic nerve, see one day.

▼ 關鍵字：optic nerve

這一段在講瑞奇羅培茲仍有視覺神經，父母認為他未來
還有希望重見光明，同樣可知瑞奇看不見這件事。

解析

01. **(D)**　第一題問的是文章主旨，在這三個步驟之後可以得知文章重點是瑞奇羅培茲沒有眼珠，得了極罕見疾病「無眼畸形症」，所以只有 (D) The baby boy had an extremely rare condition called Anophthalmia, so he has no eyeballs. 最符合文章主旨。

02. **(B)**　第二題問醫院在瑞奇的眼窩中裝膨脹器的原因，在最後一段可知原因是準備在未來裝義眼，所以答案是 (B) Because they wanted to help his sockets grow big enough to hold prosthetic eyes.。

 **必學詞彙**

» **swollen** adj. 腫起來的

» **traumatic**
adj. 痛苦難忘的；造成
創傷的

» **eyelid** n. 眼皮

» **eyeball** n. 眼球

» **rare** adj. 罕見的

» **optimistic** adj. 樂觀的

» **prosthetic**
adj. 義肢的；假體的

 **文法觀念**

1. <u>The baby Richie Lopez had an MRI 13 days later, and the traumatic</u> <u>discovery was that his eyelids weren't open because he had no</u> <u>eyeballs **beneath** those closed lids</u>— <u>an extremely rare condition</u> <u>**called Anophthalmia**.</u>

   - Beneath 通常用來表示某事物在另一事物的正下方，例：We rested beneath the willow this afternoon. 我們今天下午在垂柳下休息。

   - Called 的意思是「被稱為；叫做」，屬於被動式的用法，因此動詞要寫成過去式，例：I have a cat called Garfield. 我有一隻貓叫加菲。

2. <u>**Nevertheless**, Kelly Lopez and her husband are still optimistic that</u> <u>science will progress **enough** to help Richie, who does have an</u> <u>optic nerve, see one day.</u>

   - Nevertheless 是副詞，也可作連接詞使用，可以放在句首，放在句中時，前方必須加上逗號或分號，例：The plot of this movie was predictable; nevertheless it was entertaining. 這部電影雖然了無新意，但依然具有娛樂性。

   - Enough 的意思是「足夠地」，直接接續在動詞之後，或是形容詞和副詞之後，例：This pizza is not big enough for the three of us. 這個披薩不夠我們三個人吃。

無眼畸型症

　　當懷孕過程正常的凱莉羅培茲，在亞利桑那州的梅薩生下她的男寶寶時，她對她的寶寶沒有張開眼睛這件事，並沒有想太多，而亞利桑那 Banner Desert 醫學中心的醫護人員一開始以為這個新生兒的臉不過是腫起來而已。

　　寶寶瑞奇羅培茲在十三天後做了核磁共振造影，令人傷痛地發現，他的眼皮之所以沒有打開，是因為在那些闔上的眼皮之下，根本沒有眼球，這是一個稱為「無眼畸形症」的極罕見情況。

　　羅培茲說：「我腦中閃過的第一個想法是，這怎麼可能發生，還有為什麼竟然沒有被發現？」然而，凱莉羅培茲和她先生仍然很樂觀，他們相信將來有一天，科學會進步到足以幫助的確有一組視覺神經的瑞奇，重見光明。

　　這個三個月大的寶寶已經動過手術，將膨脹器縫入眼窩中，如此一來，它們就會一直生長到足以在將來支撐住一個義眼。

The "Death with Dignity" Law

Brittany Maynard, a 29-year-old terminally ill woman, endedher own life by taking lethal drugs made available under Oregon's "death with dignity" law. Reviving a national debate about physician-assisted dying, Maynard ended her suffering from brain cancer, and passed away in the arms of her husband, Dan Diaz, on November 1 as she planned.

After being diagnosed with terminal brain cancer, GlioblastomaMultiforme (GBM), and was given six months to live, Maynard and her husband moved to Portland from northern California so that she could take advantage of the Oregon law to end her life with dignity.

Maynard suffered increasingly frequent and longer seizures,severe head and neck pain, and stroke-like symptoms. As symptoms grew more severe, she chose to abbreviate the dying process by taking the aid-in-dying medication.

Maynard said that her husband and other relatives accepted her decision. "It's not a fear-based choice; it's a logic-based choice," she said. "There isn't a single person that loves me that wishes me more pain and more suffering."

___ 01. What's the main idea of this article?
   (A) Brittany Maynard was diagnosed with terminal brain cancer.
   (B) Brittany Maynard suffered from seizures, severe head and neck pain, and stroke-like symptoms.
   (C) Brittany Maynard decided to take lethal drugs to end her own life.
   (D) Brittany Maynard and her husband moved to Oregon, Portland.

___ 02. Why did Brittany Maynard decide to end her own life?
   (A) Because she was suicidal.
   (B) Because she wanted to take drugs.
   (C) Because she wanted to abbreviate her dying process.
   (D) Because she had a stroke.

 解題技巧 ────────

抓頭

1. **抓主題句** 掌握主題句最快的方式就是抓主詞跟動詞,可以很粗略的知道這篇文章的方向為何。

↳ 主題句:

> Brittany Maynard, a 29-year-old terminally ill woman, ended her own life by taking lethal drugs made available under Oregon's "death with dignity" law.

▼ 關鍵字:

① 主詞:Brittany Maynard　② 動詞:ended
在這篇文章中,從主題句可以掌握的是 Brittany Maynard 和她結束自己的生命。

▼ 其他資訊:29-year-old, terminally ill

29-year-old, terminally ill 是補充說明主詞 Brittany Maynard 的年齡和遭遇(得到絕症)。

2. **抓末段重點** 了解第一段後快速掃描最後一段，因為最後
一段是結尾，看完最後一段的主題句就可以
粗略了解文章的走向。

↳ 主題句：

> Maynard said that her husband and other relatives
> accepted her decision.

▼ 關鍵字：decision

文章末段提到布蘭妮梅納的丈夫和家人都支持她的決
定，能看到是她結束自己生命這個決定。

3. **抓各段的主題句**：

↳ 主題句：

> After being diagnosed with terminal brain cancer,
> Glioblastoma Multiforme (GBM), and was given six months
> to live, Maynard and her husband moved to Portland from
> northern California so that she could take advantage of the
> Oregon law to end her life with dignity.

▼ 關鍵字：terminal brain cancer

這一段在講布蘭妮梅納被診斷出腦癌後，決定搬到奧勒
岡進行尊嚴死，同樣能看出她決定結束生命的意圖和原
因。

解析

01. **(C)** 第一題問的是文章主旨，在這三個步驟之後可以得知文章重點是布蘭妮梅納得到腦癌並決定尊嚴赴死，所以只有 (C) Brittany Maynard decided to take lethal drugs to end her own life. 最符合文章主旨。

02. **(C)** 第二題問布蘭妮梅納結束生命的原因，從各段的主題句看出她結束生命的原因是她想要帶著尊嚴赴死，也就是縮短死亡的過程，所以可以推得答案是 (C) Because she wanted to abbreviate her dying process.。

必學詞彙

» **lethal**
adj. 致命的；危險的

» **dignity**
n. 尊嚴；尊貴；高尚

» **debate**
n. 辯論；討論；爭論

» **terminal** adj. 末端的；末期的

» **seizure**
n. （病的）發作

» **severe**
adj. 嚴重的；劇烈的

» **symptom**
n. 症狀；徵兆

 **文法觀念**

1. Reviving a national debate about physician-assisted dying, Maynard ended her suffering from brain cancer, **and passed** away in the arms of her husband, Dan Diaz, on November 1 **as** she planned.

   - passing 的用法，在寫長句時，可以在主句後加逗號，連接下一句話（下一個動作），這時候動詞必須寫成動名詞（V-ing），例：My mom put flour and water in a bowl, mixing away to combine. 媽媽把麵粉和水放進碗裡，攪拌均勻。

   - As 有許多種用法，在此作為連接詞，是「如同；依照」的意思，例：Children don't do as they are told. 小孩不會按照他人吩咐的做。

2. "It's not a **fear-based** choice-it's a **logic-based** choice," she said. "There isn't a single person that loves me that wishes me more pain and more suffering."

   - fear-based 和 logic-based 是複合形容詞，複合形容詞結合形容詞和動詞，變成帶有動作的形容詞，文中這兩個形容詞屬於名詞—過去分詞的型態，其它的例子有 wind-powered 風力的、sun-dried 曬乾的、money-driven 受錢驅使的。

 **中文翻譯**

尊嚴死法案

廿九歲的癌末女子布蘭妮梅納，服用在奧勒岡州的「尊嚴死法」案下被允許製造的致命藥物，結束自己的生命。挑起全國對醫師協助死亡這項議題的爭論的梅納，在她所計劃的十一月一日這天，結束了她腦癌的痛苦，在丈夫丹迪亞茲的懷中逝世。

在被診斷出罹患末期腦癌—多形性膠質母細胞瘤，並且被告知只有六個月可活之後，梅納和她的丈夫從北加州搬到波特蘭，就是為了利用奧勒岡的法律，讓自己有尊嚴地結束生命。

越來越頻繁且持久的發病、劇烈的頭頸疼痛及類似中風的症狀，讓梅納飽受痛苦。隨著症狀越來越嚴重，她選擇接受幫助死亡的藥物，來縮短死亡的過程。

梅納說她的先生和其他家人都接受她的決定。「這不是一個出於恐懼的選擇，而是個出於邏輯的選擇。」梅那說：「沒有一個愛我的人希望我承受更多的痛苦和折磨。」

09

Unmade Beds may Keep You Healthy

A Kingston University study finds that failing to make your bed in the morning may actually help keep you healthy. The research discovered that an unmade bed is unappealing to house dust mites, which can produce allergens that cause asthma and other allergies.

The scientists found that while the creatures enjoy the warm, damp conditions created in an occupied bed, they are less likely to survive and thrive when moisture is in shorter supply.

According to researcher Dr. Stephen Pretlove, mites can only survive by taking in water from the atmosphere, so leaving a bed unmade during the day can remove moisture from the sheets and mattress; then, the mites will dehydrate and eventually die.

Professor Andrew Wardlaw of the British Society for Allergy and Clinical Immunology said, "Mites are very important in asthma and allergy, and it would be good if ways were found to modify the home so that mite concentrations were reduced."

___ 01. What's the main idea of this article?
   (A) An unmade bed is unappealing to mites.
   (B) We shouldn't make our beds in the morning.
   (C) Dusts and mites can cause asthma and other allergies.
   (D) Mites enjoy warm, damp conditions.

___ 02. How come not making our beds in the morning may keep us healthy?
(A) Because it can save us time and energy.
(B) Because an unmade bed do not attract mites.
(C) Because an unmade bed can remove moisture from the sheets and mattress, making mites dehydrate and die.
(D) Because we feel happier not making our beds.

 解題技巧

抓頭

1. **抓主題句** 掌握主題句最快的方式就是抓主詞跟動詞，可以很粗略的知道這篇文章的方向為何。

↳ 主題句：

> A Kingston University study finds that <u>failing to make your bed in the morning</u> may actually help <u>keep you healthy</u>.

▼ 關鍵字：
① 主詞：failing to make your bed in the morning
② 動詞：keep you healthy
在這篇文章中，從主題句可以掌握的是不整理床和健康。

▼ 其他資訊：
A Kingston University study 是補充說明這項論點的來源。

抓尾

2. **抓末段重點** 了解第一段後快速掃描最後一段，因為最後一段是結尾，看完最後一段的主題句就可以粗略了解文章的走向。

↳ 主題句：

> Mites are very important in asthma and allergy, and it would be good if ways were found to modify the home so that mite concentrations were reduced.

▼ 關鍵字：Mites

文章末段提到塵蟎對人體帶來的影響，可看出文章在探討整理床和塵蟎之間的關係。

3. **抓各段的主題句**：

↳ 主題句：

> The scientists found that while the creatures enjoy the warm, damp conditions created in an occupied bed, they are less likely to survive and thrive when moisture is in shorter supply.

▼ 關鍵字：in shorter supply

這一段在講室內塵蟎在濕氣較低時，較無法存活及繁殖，同樣能看出文章著墨於整理床和塵蟎間的關係。

解析

01. **(A)** 第一題問的是文章主旨，在這三個步驟之後可以得知文章重點是塵蟎不喜歡沒有整理的床，所以只有 (A) An unmade bed is unappealing to mites. 最符合文章主旨。

02. **(C)** 第二題問不整理床為何能替我們保持健康，根據文章第三段，研究者說塵蟎靠吸收空氣中的水分才能存活，沒有整理的床不利於塵蟎存活，所以答案是 (C) Because an unmade bed can remove moisture from the sheets and mattress, making mites dehydrate and die.。

必學詞彙

- » **unmade**
  adj. 尚未整理的
- » **unappealing**
  adj. 無感染力的；不吸引人的
- » **allergy** n. 過敏症

- » **survive** v. 存活
- » **thrive** v. 繁盛；興旺
- » **moisture**
  n. 濕氣；水分
- » **occupied**
  adj. 在使用的；已占用的

 **文法觀念**

1. According to researcher Dr. Stephen Pretlove, mites can only survive by taking in water from the atmosphere, so **leaving** a bed **unmade during** the day can remove moisture from the sheets and mattress so the mites will dehydrate and eventually die.

   - Leave...un- 是個很常見的用語，leave 是「離開；放著」的意思，而後方的形容詞 unmade 是「沒有整理」，un 後方加上過去分詞，表示狀態，此類用語常見的有 leave...unsaid 還沒有說、leave...undone 還沒有做，例句：Please do not leave your bags unattended at the airport. 在機場時，請要看好自己的包包。

   - During 為介系詞，後方通常接名詞，是「在……期間」的意思，用來表示時間，例：Amy went to Italy with her family during the summer vacation. 艾咪暑假跟家人去義大利玩。

2. "Mites are very important in asthma and allergy and it would be good if ways were found to modify the home **so that** mite concentrations were reduced."

   - So that 是副詞連接詞，表達「因此；以至於」的意思，同時也連接上下兩個句子，例：I adopted the cat so that she can have a home. 我領養了那隻貓，讓她有個家。

沒整理的床有助健康

一份金斯頓大學的研究發現，早上不整理床，其實可能會幫你保持健康。這項研究發現：會製造引發氣喘和其他過敏症的過敏原的室內塵蟎，很不喜歡沒有整理的床。

科學家發現，雖然這些生物喜歡使用中的床鋪所製造的溫暖潮濕環境，但是牠們在濕氣較低時，比較無法存活及繁殖。

研究者史提芬普列特羅夫表示：塵蟎只有靠吸收空氣中的水分才能存活，所以白天把床放著不整理，可以移除床單和床墊上的濕氣，如此一來塵蟎就會脫水，最後死亡。

英國過敏及臨床免疫學會的安德魯瓦羅教授表示，「塵蟎是導致氣喘及過敏症的重要來源，能找到改變居家環境，減少塵蟎集中的方法，是件好事。」

Range-R

Dozens of U.S. police departments and law enforcement agencies have deployed radar systems, known as Range-R, inside American homes that allow them to look through walls and search homes from the outside. A Range-R uses radio waves to focus its gaze on movements to examine from up to 50 feet away and through walls whether someone is present.

The practice, which law enforcement agencies have been loath to talk about, was disclosed when a federal judge in Denver was informed that police used one before entering a house to apprehend a man accused of violating his parole.

"The idea that the government can send signals throughthe wall of your house to figure out whether anything inside is problematic," said the principal technologist at the American Civil Liberties Range-R Lets Police See through Walls and Know if You're Home Union, "Technologies like that are among the intrusive tools that police have."

While privacy advocates are expressing concern, Federal officials persisted that the Range-R technology is necessary to keep officers safe as Marshals Service routinely pursues and arrests violent offenders.

___ 01. According to the article, what is the purpose of Range-R technology?
  (A) To help the police solve crimes.
  (B) To let the police spy on every citizen.
  (C) To let the police look through walls and search homes from the outside.
  (D) To control citizens' freedom.

___ 02. Why are people concerned about Range-R technology?
  (A) Because it is an invasion of privacy.
  (B) Because they want to protect criminals.
  (C) Because they don't like the police departments.
  (D) Because they think radio waves are harmful to their health.

 解題技巧 ─────────────

抓
頭

1. **抓主題句** 掌握主題句最快的方式就是抓主詞跟動詞，可以很粗略的知道這篇文章的方向為何。

↳ 主題句：

> Dozens of U.S. police departments and law enforcement agencies have deployed radar systems, known as Range-R, inside American homes that allow them to look through walls and search homes from the outside.

▼ 關鍵字：

① 主詞：U.S. police departments and law enforcement agencies

② 動詞：deployed radar systems

在這篇文章中，從主題句可以掌握的是，美國警察局和執法機關和運用雷達系統。

▼ 其他資訊：

① Dozens of 是補充說明主詞 U.S. police departments and law enforcement agencies。

② 這項科技被稱為 Range-R。

2. **抓末段重點** 了解第一段後快速掃描最後一段，因為最後一段是結尾，看完最後一段的主題句就可以粗略了解文章的走向。

↳ 主題句：

> While privacy advocates are <u>expressing concern</u>, Federal officials persisted that the Range-R technology is necessary to keep officers safe as Marshals Service routinely pursues and arrests violent offenders.

▼ 關鍵字：expressing concern

文章末段提到隱私權擁護者對此表達擔憂，可看出這是一項具有爭議性的科技。

3. 抓各段的主題句：

↳ 主題句：

> The practice, which law enforcement agencies have been loath to talk about, was disclosed when a federal judge in Denver was informed that police used one before entering a house to <u>apprehend a man</u> accused of violating his parole.

▼ 關鍵字：apprehend a man

這一段在講警方曾經運用 Range-R 技術，逮捕一名被控違反假釋規定的男子，能看出警方採用 Range-R 技術有其原因。

解析

01. **(C)** 第一題問的是 Range-R 技術的用途，從第一段的後半部和第二段舉例說明，警方曾以此技術逮捕被控違反假釋的男子，可以判斷出答案是 (C) To let the police look through walls and search homes from the outside.。

02. **(A)** 第二題問民眾為何對此項技術有顧慮，倒數第二段中，美國公民自由聯盟的總技術師說，這是一項侵入性工具，以及末段提到隱私權擁護者對此表達擔憂，可得知答案是 (A) Because it is an invasion of privacy.。

必學詞彙

» **search** v. 搜查；探查

» **examine** v. 檢查；細查

» **disclose** v. 透露；揭發

» **apprehend** v. 逮捕

» **problematic**
   adj. 有很多問題的；不確定的

» **intrusive**
   adj. 侵入的；干擾的

» **necessary**
   adj. 有必要的

 **文法觀念**

1. Dozens of U.S. police departments and law enforcement agencies have deployed radar systems, **known as** Range-R, inside American homes that allow them to look through walls and search homes from the outside.

    - Dozens of 在此是「許多的；大批的」的意思，當 dozen 前方擺了數字，dozen 這個字就不可以再加 s，例：I got two dozen eggs from the farm. 我跟農場買了兩打雞蛋。

    - Known as，known 的後面加上 for、to、as 各有不同的意思，加上 as 則是「以某個身分出名」的意思，例：Elvis Presley is known as "The King of Rock 'n' Roll." 艾維斯普利斯萊被喻為「搖滾樂之王」。

2. A Range-R uses radio waves to focus its gaze on movements to examine from up to 50 feet away and through walls **whether** someone is present.

    - Whether 用在討論「是否」的句子裡，後方連接子句，例：I am not sure whether he likes me or not. 我不確定他是否喜歡我。

3. "Technologies like that are **among** the intrusive tools that police have."

    - Among 用來表達「在⋯⋯之間」，不是在兩者之間，而是處於⋯⋯之間，具有整體性的概念，例：The cabin is hidden among the woods. 小木屋深藏於森林間。

中文翻譯

穿牆雷達

　　很多美國警察局和執法機關，已經在美國家庭中部署了一種稱為 Range-R 的雷達系統，讓他們能夠透視牆壁，從外面搜查屋內的狀況。Range-R 是利用無線電波將光束集中在動作上，可從五十呎以外的地方穿透牆壁，檢查是不是有人在裡面。

　　一名丹佛聯邦法官得知，有警察在進入一間屋子逮捕被控違反假釋規定的男子前，使用這項裝置，因而揭露了這個執法機關一直不願意談論的做法。

　　「讓政府可以穿透你家的牆壁輸送信號，以得知裡面有什麼東西，這樣的想法是很有問題的，」美國公民自由聯盟的總技術師說：「像那樣的科技是警方所擁有的侵入性工具。」

　　儘管隱私權擁護者表達了關切，美國聯邦政府官員堅稱，因為執法人員經常要追捕暴力的違法者，因此 Range-R 技術對警察的安全是有必要的。

11

The Application of Network: Big Data

Big data and predictive analytics are a great fit for the modern data center and IT operations. The approaches and systems found within big data is helpful in dealing with the great deal of data being generated within IT operations.

In a post titled "Use Big Network Data to Predict and Avoid Network Problems", Scott Koegler describes the use of data analysis and predictive analytics as "By turning predictive analytics inward to track where breaks happen most frequently, IT and network admins can set more accurate thresholds for recurring issues, positioning themselves ahead of any damages."

Predictive analytics and other big data approaches not only allow IT operations to understand and predict when breaks or issues might arise within the data center, network or remote office, but also help to identify bottlenecks, manage incidents and fix issues faster. For example, an IT specialist in a central office can get a notification that something in a branch office is amiss, and the notification can provide a recommendation to "fix" the problem before it actually becomes a problem.

___ 01. What's the main idea of this article?
   (A) Predictive analytics and other big data approaches allow IT operations to understand and predict potential issues.
   (B) Scott Koegler wrote a post titled "Use Big Network Data to Predict and Avoid Network Problems".
   (C) Big data and predictive analytics are very helpful to modern data center and IT operations.
   (D) With big data and predictive analytics, IT specialist in a central office can get a notification when something goes wrong in a branch office.

___ 02. According to the article, what is not the use of data analysis and predictive analytics?
   (A) To understand issues better.
   (B) To position IT and network admins ahead of any damages.
   (C) To manage incidents.
   (D) To replace IT specialists.

 解題技巧 ─────────────

1. **抓主題句** 掌握主題句最快的方式就是抓主詞跟動詞，可以很粗略的知道這篇文章的方向為何。

抓
頭

↳ 主題句：

> Big data and predictive analytics <u>are a great fit</u> for the modern data center and IT operations.

▼ 關鍵字：

① 主詞：Big data and predictive analytics
② 動詞：are a great fit
在這篇文章中，從主題句可以掌握的是大數據及預言性分析與其用處。

2. **抓末段重點** 了解第一段後快速掃描最後一段，因為最後
　　　　　　 一段是結尾，看完最後一段的主題句就可以
　　　　　　 粗略了解文章的走向。

↳ 主題句：

> 　　Predictive analytics and other big data approaches not only allow IT operations to understand and predict when breaks or issues might arise within the data center, network or remote office, but also help to <u>identify bottlenecks</u>, <u>manage incidents,</u> and <u>fix issues faster.</u>

▼ 關鍵字：identify bottlenecks, manage incidents and fix
　　　　　　issues faster

文章末段提到預言性分析及其他大數據方法的許多作用。

3. **抓各段的主題句**：

↳ 主題句：

> 　　"By turning predictive analytics inward to track where breaks happen most frequently, IT and network admins can set more accurate thresholds for recurring issues, positioning themselves <u>ahead of any damages</u>."

▼ 關鍵 ：ahead of any damages

這一段在講資訊技術及網路管理人員能如何運用預言性分析，以及預言性分析及其他大數據的多用途。

抓
尾

補
強

解析

01. **(C)**　第一題問的是文章主旨，在這三個步驟之後可以得知，文章重點是預言性分析及大數據的益處，所以 (C) Big data and predictive analytics are very helpful to modern data center and IT operations. 最符合文章主旨。

02. **(D)**　第二題問哪個選項不是大數據的用途，文章裡敘述大數據能如何替資訊技術專員解決問題，而非取代他們，所以答案是 (D) To replace IT specialists.。

 必學詞彙

» **data** n. 資料；數據

» **approach** n. 方法；門徑

» **track** v. 追蹤

» **predict** v. 預測；預料

» **identify** v. 確認；識別

» **notification** n. 通知；通告；通知書

» **recommendation** n. 勸告；建議

 **文法觀念**

1. The approaches and systems found **within** big data is helpful in dealing with the great deal of data being generated within IT operations.

   - Within 常作介系詞，意思是「在⋯⋯之間；在⋯⋯之內」，用來限定時間範圍，後方接名詞，例：I will get back to you within a week. 我一星期之內會回覆你。

2. "By turning predictive analytics inward to track where breaks happen most frequently, IT and network admins can set more accurate thresholds for recurring issues, positioning themselves ahead of **any** damages."

   - Any 是量詞之一，後方通常接複數可數名詞，也可接單數名詞，用意、語氣不同，但在問句中，例：「Are there any books for me to read? 有書能讓我看嗎？」；或「Any sensible person will agree that bullying people is wrong. 任何明智的人都會同意霸凌他人是錯的。」

3. For example, an IT specialist in a central office can get a notification that something in a branch office is amiss, and the notification can provide a recommendation to "fix" the problem **before** it actually becomes a problem.

   - Before 為連接詞，用來表達時間關連，並連接上下子句，before 可擺句首、句中或句尾。擺在句首時，子句之間要加上逗號，例：Before Kevin went to bed, he took a shower. 凱文洗了澡才上床睡覺。

 **中文翻譯**

網路大數據的應用

　　大數據及預言性分析超適合用在現代數據中心及資訊技術操作上。在大數據中發現的方法和系統，對處理資訊技術操作中所產生的大量資訊極有幫助。

　　在標題為「利用大網路數據預測並避免網路問題」一文中，史考特寇格勒描述數據分析及預言性分析為「利用預言性分析內轉，頻繁地追蹤錯誤發生之處的方式，資訊技術及網路管理人員便能為重複發生的問題，設定更精確的門檻，使它們能夠預防可能發生的損壞。」

　　預言性分析及其他大數據方法，不僅讓資訊技術操作能了解並預測數據中心、網路系統或偏遠辦公室中可能發生的問題，也有助於辨識瓶頸、管理突發狀況，並更快速地修復問題。舉例來說，一個在中央辦公室的資訊技術專員可以收到分公司出現錯誤的通知，而該通知也能在錯誤確實成為問題前，提供「修復」問題的建議。

12

Fashion Party Invitation

From: Mr. Daniel Watson (Director of Daisy & Daniel's)

To: Mr. Thomas Rodman

Subject: Business Event Invitation

Date: 2020-04-12

Dear Mr. Rodman,

I hope that this letter finds you in the best of health and spirit. As you are among our valued customer, we would like to thank you for your business and would take this opportunity to invite you for the launch of our new apparel series on 10th of May, 2020 at 5 p.m. at Hotel Regent.

An opening ceremony and then a dinner party are organized just to extend our gratitude to our guests. We want to introduce our new line of fashion apparel to our valued clients and customers, so we want all our guests to attend the party.

Please give us your confirmation by 30th of April, 2020.

Your presence is thus sought for.

Sincerely Yours,

Daniel Watson

From: Mr. Thomas Rodman

To: Mr. Daniel Watson

Subject: Re: Business Event Invitation

Dear Daniel,

Thanks for your kind invitation. Unfortunately, due to a prior commitment on the date of your function, I regret that I will be unable to attend the opening ceremony.

Please accept my sincere congratulations on the launch of your new apparel series.

Hope we could arrange a time to get together after the celebration.

Yours,

Thomas Rodman

___ 01. What can we learn from the e-mails?
  (A) Mr. Rodman was invited to Mr. Watson's wedding ceremony.
  (B) Mr. Rodman declined the invitation because of a prior engagement.
  (C) There will be a press conference at Hotel Regent.
  (D) Mr. Rodman will attend the ceremony in person.

___ 02. On which of the following dates is the responding e-mail most likely to be sent?
  (A) 28th of April, 2020.　　(B) 10th of May, 2020.
  (C) 28th of May, 2020.　　(D) 10th of April, 2020.

___ 03. According to the emails, what is the relation between Mr. Rodman and Mr. Watson?

(A) They are employer and employee.

(B) They are old family friends.

(C) They are distant relatives.

(D) They have dealings in business.

 解題技巧 ────────────────

<table>
<tr>
<td rowspan="1">抓
頭</td>
<td>

1. <u>抓主題句</u> 掌握主題句最快的方式就是抓主詞跟動詞，可以很粗略的知道這篇文章的方向為何。

↳ 主題句：

> we would like to thank you for your business and would take this opportunity to invite you for the launch of our new apparel series on 10th of May, 2020 at 5 p.m. at Hotel Regent.

▼ 關鍵字：

① 主詞：we ② 動詞：invite

在這篇文章中，從主題句可以掌握的是寄件人和邀請。

▼ 其他資訊：the launch

the launch 補充說明主詞 we 的邀請內容。

</td>
</tr>
<tr>
<td>抓
尾</td>
<td>

2. <u>抓末段重點</u> 了解第一段後快速掃描最後一段，因為最後一段是結尾，看完最後一段的主題句就可以粗略了解文章的走向。

↳ 主題句：

> I regret that I will be <u>unable</u> to attend the opening ceremony.

</td>
</tr>
</table>

▼ 關鍵字：unable

文章末段是湯瑪斯的回覆，他無法出席活動。

補
強

3. **抓各段的主題句：**

↳ 主題句：

> Please give us your <u>confirmation</u> by 30th of April, 2020.

▼ 關鍵字：confirmation

這段是丹尼爾請湯瑪斯回覆，能看出丹尼爾寄出了某種邀約。

解析

01. **(B)** 第一題問哪個選項是正確的，在第二封郵件能看到湯瑪斯活動當天有其他約會，所以答案是 (B) Mr. Rodman declined the invitation because of a prior engagement.。

02. **(A)** 第二題問回覆的郵件最可能在何時寄出，丹尼爾請湯瑪斯在四月三十日前回覆，所以答案是 (A) 28th of April, 2020.。

03. **(D)** 第三題問兩人之間的關係，從第一封郵件可看到丹尼爾說湯瑪斯是公司最尊貴的客戶之一，可看出兩人之間有商業來往，因此，答案是 (D) They have dealings in business.。

文法觀念

1. Your presence is thus sought for.

   • Thus 是副詞，意思是「藉此；因此；於是」，thus 經常出現在學術文章中，例如：Families struggling to make ends meet are thus less likely to send their kids to university. 難以維持生計的家庭就更不可能送孩子去上大學了。

2. Unfortunately, due to a prior commitment on the date of your function, I regret that I will be unable to attend the opening ceremony.

   • Due to 是介系詞，後方一定要接續名詞，due to 常用來表達原因，意思是「因為；由於」，例如：They suffer Poverty from due to the lack of education. 他們會貧窮是因為缺乏教育。

 **必學詞彙**

» **gratitude** n. 感恩；感謝	» **presence** n. 出席，在場；存在
» **confirmation** n. 確定；確證；確認	» **opportunity** n. 機會
» **arrange** v. 整理；安排	» **ceremony** n. 儀式，典禮
» **valued** adj. 貴重的；寶貴的	

 **中文翻譯**

時尚派對邀請

寄件人：丹尼爾華森先生（Daisy & Daniel's 負責人）
收件人：湯瑪斯羅德曼先生
主旨：商業活動邀請
日期：2020-04-12
親愛的羅德曼先生，

　　希望您收到信時身體與精神都處於最佳狀態。您是我們尊貴的客戶之一，我們想要感謝您的光顧，並藉此機會邀請您參加我們的新裝系列發表會，2020 年五月十日下午五點在麗晶飯店。

　　我們準備了開幕式與晚餐派對以感謝我們的顧客。我們想介紹我們新的時裝系列給我們尊貴的代理商與顧客，所以希望所有人都能參加這個派對。

　　請於 2020 年四月三十日前與我們確認。

　　由衷盼望您的蒞臨。
丹尼爾華森　敬上

寄件人：湯瑪斯羅德曼先生
收件人：丹尼爾華森先生
主旨：回覆：商業活動邀請
親愛的丹尼爾，

　　感謝您善意的邀請。不巧地，您舉辦活動當天我已有其他安排，我恐怕沒辦法參加您的開幕式。

　　請接受我誠摯的向您祝賀新時裝系列的發表。

　　希望慶祝會後我們可以另外約個時間聚聚。
湯瑪斯羅德曼　敬上

13
The Internet of Things

IOT (The Internet of Things) may be the next big thing in appliances. At the 2015 CES show, Samsung CEO B.K. Yoon announced that 90 percent of the devices his company sells will connect to the Internet by 2020.

The Internet of Things could include every electronic device in your home, from door locks to cell phones, coffee makers to toasters.

Your appliances will not only be computerized, but also be connected to each other and the Internet. With a single type of microcontroller across a range of appliances, you can simply reprogram for the task at hand. The system on a chip (SoC) can control the function of the devices, turning on or off the pumps and valves in your refrigerator, or mixing the hot and cold water in your washing machine to reach the right wash temperature.

As Appliance Science looks at the science and technology behind the Internet of Things, we can expect to be surrounded by a cloud of chatty appliances and other devices, all talking among themselves, in just a few years.

___ 01. What's the main idea of this article?
    (A) 90 percent of the devices Samsung sells will connect to the Internet by 2020.
    (B) In the future, home appliances will not only be connected to each other but also the Internet.
    (C) There will be appliances that can talk in the future.
    (D) With the system on a chip, you can control things like refrigerators and washing machines.

___ 02. What might The Internet of Things be connected to?
    (A) A refrigerator.   (B) A car.   (C) A letterbox.   (D) A sofa.

 解題技巧

抓
頭

1. **抓主題句** 掌握主題句最快的方式就是抓主詞跟動詞，可以很粗略的知道這篇文章的方向為何。

↳ 主題句：

> IOT (The Internet of Things) <u>may be the next big thing in</u> appliances.

▼ 關鍵字：

① 主詞：IOT　② 動詞：may be the next big thing

在這篇文章中，從主題句可以掌握到物聯網可能成為下一件大事。

▼ 其他資訊：

in appliances 是補充說明主詞 IOT 物聯網在家電用品這個區塊的情況。

2. **抓末段重點** 了解第一段後快速掃描最後一段，因為最後
一段是結尾，看完最後一段的主題句就可以
粗略了解文章的走向。

↳ 主題句：

> As Appliance Science looks at the science and technology
> behind the Internet of Things, we can expect to be surrounded
> by a cloud of chatty appliances and other devices, all talking
> among themselves, in just a few years.

▼ **關鍵字**：a cloud of chatty appliances

文章末段提到我們將來可以預期生活中圍繞著會說話的
家電用品。

3. **抓各段的主題句**：

↳ 主題句：

> Your appliances will not only be computerized, but also
> be connected to each other and the Internet.

▼ **關鍵字**：connected

這一段在講家電用品不但會被電腦化，還會與彼此和網
路互相連結，同樣能看到物聯網的概念。

解析

01. **(B)**　第一題問的是文章主旨，在這三個步驟之後可以得知文章重點是物聯網，所以只有 (B) In the future, home appliances will not only be connected to each other but also the Internet. 最符合文章主旨。

02. **(A)**　第二題問物聯網能連結到什麼，文章的第二段 The Internet of Things could include every <u>electronic device</u> in your home, from door locks to cell phones, coffee makers to toasters. ，說明物聯網能連結到家電用品，選項中只有 (A) A refrigerator 是家電用品，所以可以推得答案是 (A)。

必學詞彙

» **appliance**
n. 器具；用具；裝置

» **connect** v. 連接；連結

» **electronic** adj. 電子的

» **device** n. 儀器；裝置

» **computerized**
adj. 電腦化的

» **reprogram**
v. 改編（電腦程序）

» **chatty**
adj. 聊天般的；饒舌的

 **文法觀念**

1. <u>The Internet of Things could include **every** electronic device in</u> <u>your home, **from** door locks **to** cell phones, coffee makers to</u> <u>toasters.</u>

    - Every 為限定詞,用來限定範圍,是「每個」的意思,後方只能連接單數名詞,例:May has been to every concert of her favorite band. 梅參加過她最愛的樂團舉辦的每一場演唱會。

    - From...to 是「從……到……」的意思,from 經常和 to 合用,可以連接地點、事物或是人,例:John walked from his house to Taipei 101. 約翰從家裡走到臺北 101。

2. <u>With a single type of microcontroller **across** a range of appliances,</u> <u>you can simply reprogram for the task at hand.</u>

    - Across 是「交叉;穿越過某處;橫跨」的意思,常用於實際穿越某處,但文中的句子裡,across 代表的是「橫跨整個系列」的概念,例:There are 14 colors across the new collection. 新系列裡有 14 個顏色。

物聯網

物聯網可能是家電用品的下一件大事。在 2015 年的國際消費電子展上，三星集團總裁尹富根宣布，在 2020 年之前，他們公司百分之九十所售出的商品將能與網路連結。

物聯網可能包含你家中所有的電器用品，從門鎖到手機，從咖啡機到烤麵包機。

你的家電用品不但會被電腦化，而且還會與彼此和網路互相連結。只要有一個能遙控一系列家電的微控制器，你就能隨手重新設定家電任務。系統單晶片可以控制器具們的功能，開關你家冰箱的幫浦和氣閥，或是調和洗衣機的冷熱水，使之達到正確的洗衣溫度。

正因為家電用品科技注目著物聯網背後的科技，可預期在未來幾年之內，我們將被一群會說話並彼此聊天的家電及其他用品所包圍。

14

What Does a Geologist Do?

If you are an adventurous person and undecided what field you want to study, you could do worse than to consider Geology. While on the face of it, the study of rocks may not sound inviting, the reality is rather different. Have you ever watched a documentary channel, as a volcano erupts massive amounts of lava, the camera pans to a crazy person, dwarfed by the size of the eruption, bravely collecting a sample amid the gas and heat? Almost certainly that person is a geologist. If that sounds a bit too hot, then imagine another common picture. Somewhere close to the pole, ice and snow cover the scene from horizon to horizon. A lonely figure moves slowly across the frozen waste to a rock outcrop somewhere. Ask this polar explorer what his job is, and more than likely he, too, is a Geologist. For some people who might not be that adventurous at heart, living on the edge in some of the harshest climate is a little too hectic. Considering this scenario, a group of people sit around large monitors in a darkened room. On the displays is the surface of Mars, and with their computers they are controlling a vehicle millions of kilometers away. They work as a team to decide where it goes and what it does. With it, they use its instruments to probe the chemical make-up of the planet, and from that, attempt to answer one of the most fundamental questions—Is there life on another world? And what do these people seeking life on mars study? It's Geology. Of course some geologists do just work in a laboratory, peering at minerals with a microscope, or doing calculations to work out the acid content of a particular mineral. Such routine is much like the work of every accountant or computer programmer. But unlike most other professions, if they get a little bored with their job, they can reapply for a position where they work with satellites in orbit around another planet without having to go back to school to learn a new career.

___ 01. What field does the author suggest to choose if the adventurous person undecided?
  (A) Chemistry   (B) Biology
  (C) Geology   (D) Geography

___ 02. While a volcano erupts massive amounts of lava, who might bravely collect a sample amid the gas and heat mentioned in the text?
  (A) chemist   (B) geologist
  (C) biologist   (D) geographer

___ 03. The place close to can see the scene from horizon to horizon with ice and snow?
  (A) the pole   (B) the equator
  (C) the mountain   (D) the lake

___ 04. According to the text, what subject do people seeking life on mars study in the past?
  (A) Math   (B) Chemistry
  (C) Geography   (D) Geology

___ 05. What profession does the article mention again and again?
  (A) Professor   (B) Biologist
  (C) Geologist   (D) Geographer

解題技巧

抓頭

1. **抓主題句** 掌握主題句最快的方式就是抓主詞跟動詞,可以很粗略的知道這篇文章的方向為何。

↳ 主題句:

> If you are an adventurous person and undecided what field you want to study, you could do worse than to <u>consider Geology</u>.

▼ 關鍵字:

① 主詞:Geology　② 動詞:consider

在這篇文章中,從主題句可以掌握的是考慮攻讀地質學。

▼ 其他資訊:what field you want to study

what field you want to study 說明討論的主題是研究領域。

抓尾

2. **抓末段重點** 了解第一段後快速掃描最後一段,因為最後一段是結尾,看完最後一段的主題句就可以粗略了解文章的走向。

↳ 主題句:

> But unlike most other professions, if they get a little bored with their job, they can <u>reapply for a position</u> where they work with satellites in orbit around another planet without having to go back to school to learn a new career.

▼ 關鍵字:reapply for a position

文章末段提到地質學家能夠重新申請職位,不用改變職業,可見文章在說明研究地質學的優點。

3. <u>抓各段的主題句</u>：
↳ 主題句：

> With it, they use its instruments to probe the chemical make-up of the planet, and from that, attempt to <u>answer one of the most fundamental questions</u>—Is there life on another world? And what do these people seeking life on mars study? It's Geology.

▼ 關鍵字：answer one of the most fundamental questions
這在講地質學能替人類解答重要的問題，同樣能看出文章在說明地質學的優點。

 解析 —————————————————

01. **(C)** 第一題問不確定想要攻讀哪個領域，又喜歡冒險的人可以考慮攻讀什麼科系，從文章的主題句可以看出是地質學，所以答案是 (C) Geology。

02. **(B)** 第二題問火山爆發大量熔岩時，在一旁收集樣本的人會是誰，文章中寫道 Almost certainly that person is a geologist.，所以答案是 (B) geologist。

03. **(A)** 第三題問在哪裡會看見被冰雪層層覆蓋的大地，文章中寫道 Somewhere close to the pole, ice and snow cover the scene from horizon to horizon.，所以答案是 (A) the pole。

04. **(D)** 第四題問哪個學科領域會在火星上尋找生命體，文章中寫 And what do these people seeking life on mars study? It's Geology.，因此，答案是 (D) Geology。

05. **(C)**　第五題問文章一再提到的職業為何，看過各個主題
　　　　　句之後，可以得知文章在討論地質學家，所以答案
　　　　　是 (C) Geologist。

必學詞彙

> **adventurous**
　adj. 愛冒險的；大膽的

> **erupt** v. 噴出；爆發

> **horizon** n. 地平線

> **programer**
　n.（電腦的）程式設
　計師

> **satellite**
　n. 衛星；人造衛星

> **darkened**
　adj. 變黑的；沒有燈光
　的

> **geologist**
　n. 地質學家；地質學者

文法觀念

1. While on the face of it, the study of rocks may not sound inviting, the reality is **rather** different.

   • Rather 屬於副詞，通常是「寧願」的意思，例：I'd rather be poor than taking someone else's money. 我寧願窮也不願拿別人的錢。在本句則用來表達「相當；有一點」，例：She is rather delightful to talk to. 跟她聊天相當愉快。

2. **Such** routine is much like the work of every accountant or computer programmer.

   • Such 屬於限定詞，後方接續名詞，在本句的意思是「如此的」，例：He should be put behind bars for having committed such horrible crime. 犯下如此可怕的罪行，他該進牢裡去。

 **中文翻譯**

地質學家的工作

如果你是喜歡冒險的人，並且還不確定想要攻讀哪個領域，不如考慮地質學。雖然從表面看來，研究岩石聽起來並不吸引人，但事實卻不然。你曾經在紀錄片頻道看過火山爆發大量熔岩，攝影鏡頭轉向一個與火山爆發相比顯得矮小的狂人，勇敢地在火山氣體與高溫之中收集樣本嗎？幾乎可以確定的是，那個人必定是個地質學家。若這聽來讓你覺得有點太熱了，那麼想想另一個常見的畫面。某個接近極地之處，冰和雪層層覆蓋著大地。一個孤單的身影緩緩穿越冰冷的荒野走到某個露出礦脈的岩石。問問這個極地探險者的職業是什麼，他也極可能是一名地質學家。對某些可能不那麼愛冒險的人來說，在最嚴厲的氣候邊緣生活可能有點太辛苦了。所以，有一群考慮到這種情況的人，是坐在沒有燈光的房間裡的大螢幕前工作的。螢幕顯示的是火星表面；還有他們用電腦控制的那些數百萬公里之外的太空火箭。他們以團隊方式工作，決定太空火箭要前往何處或做些什麼。有了火箭，他們可以利用其儀器去探測該行星的化學構造，並試圖以此找到最重要的問題的答案─在另一個世界是否有生命存在？而這些在火星上尋找生命體的人們，過去攻讀的是什麼？是地質學。當然，的確有一些地質學家是只在實驗室工作的，他們用顯微鏡盯著礦物瞧，或計算某個礦物中酸的含量。這樣的例行公事就像每個會計師或電腦程式設計師的工作一樣。但與大多數其他行業不同的是，如果他們對工作稍微感到厭倦了，可以重新申請一個職位，做些關於繞在另一個星球的軌道上運轉的衛星的研究工作，而不必回到學校重新學習一門新的職業技能。

15

Some Suggestions for "Soho"

Imagine getting up from bed, brewing up a cup of your favorite coffee then drifting over to your scenic window in your condominium. You fire up PC, browse some email, type up a couple of documents and facilitate a negotiation on the phone. Then, it's time for your favorite TV show. While watching that, you quickly complete a couple of tasks and scan the email before drifting down to lunch somewhere interesting while planning your afternoon's labors. Sometimes you'll bring along the laptop and accomplish five hours worth of office work in only 45 minutes in the coffee shop, and enjoy the rest of your day with friends. Many people believe this a typical day in the life of someone who works from home. Yet, when they try it, they quickly find that they need to adapt their view to reality. More often than not, working from home is a chaotic mess of trying to get household chores done, endless emails and phone calls and an ever increasing pile of both work and personal half finished projects . Instead of working from home, home becomes work, and you never get to leave! The problem is not the volume of work, but is finding time to do it and running a household at the same time. This all stems from the fact that human beings are lousy at multitasking. So, if you work from home, heed the following advice. Separate home and work as completely as you can. Have a time for concentrating on work, and a different time to dedicate to enjoying the comforts of home. It is also helpful to have an "office" at home, however small. Designate an official office chair and table. When you need to work, go there and work. If you want a break, seat yourself elsewhere in the house. In essence, make you life as single tasked as possible. When you are doing work, be 100% there doing work. When you are not, be 100% at home relaxing. Anything in between will result in poor work performance and a frustrating home life.

___ 01. According to the article, sometimes you can accomplish _____ worth of office work in only 45 minutes in the coffee shop.
    (A) six hours   (B) seven hours
    (C) four hours   (D) five hours

___ 02. Why does working at home become a chaotic mess?
    (A) because of lots of household chores
    (B) because of endless emails
    (C) because you haven't arranged time well.
    (D) because of an increasing pile of work

___ 03. What is the author's suggestion about this?
    (A) Do the work as much as you can.
    (B) Separate home and work as completely as you can.
    (C) Focus on your personal half finished projects.
    (D) Don't separate home and work at all.

解題技巧 ————————————————————

抓頭

1. **抓主題句** 掌握主題句最快的方式就是抓主詞跟動詞，可以很粗略的知道這篇文章的方向為何。

↳ 主題句：

> More often than not, <u>working from home</u> <u>is a chaotic mess</u> of trying to get household chores done, endless emails and phone calls and an ever increasing pile of both work and personal half finished projects.

▼ 關鍵字：

① 主詞：working from home
② 動詞：is a chaotic mess
在這篇文章中，從主題句可以掌握的是在家工作和雜亂無章的狀態。

▼ 其他資訊：More often than not

More often than not 是補充說明主詞 working from home 經常變得雜亂無章（is a chaotic mess）。

抓尾

2. **抓末段重點** 了解第一段後快速掃描最後一段，因為最後一段是結尾，看完最後一段的主題句就可以粗略了解文章的走向。

↳ 主題句：

> Anything <u>in between</u> will result in poor work performance and a frustrating home life.

▼ 關鍵字：in between
文章末段提到工作和家庭生活未取得平衡的結果。

3. **抓各段的主題句**：

↳ 主題句：

> This all stems from the fact that human beings are <u>lousy at</u> <u>multitasking</u>.

▼ 關鍵字：lousy at multitasking

這在講人們不擅長同一時間做許多件事，同樣能看出文章在探討在家工作，時間和效率是很重要的。

解析

01. **(D)** 文章中寫道 Sometimes you'll bring along the laptop and accomplish <u>five hours</u> worth of office work in only 45 minutes in the coffee shop, 所以答案是 (D) five hours。

02. **(C)** 第二題問在家工作為何會變得雜亂無章，從文章中可看出時間管理的重要性，所以答案是 (C) because you haven't arranged time well.。

03. **(B)** 第三題問作者建議該如何應付這雜亂無章的情況，文章中說要將家庭生活和工作盡量澈底分開，答案是 (B) Separate home and work as completely as you can.。

必學詞彙

- » **condominium**
  n. 獨立公寓

- » **multitasking**
  n. 多工處理；多重任務處理

- » **endless**
  adj. 不斷的；無休止的

- » **chaotic** **adj.** 混亂的；無秩序的

- » **essence**
  n. 本質；實質；要素

- » **document**
  n. 公文；文件；證件

- » **designate**
  v. 標出；表明；指定

文法觀念

1. Sometimes you'll bring along the laptop and accomplish five hours **worth of** office work in only 45 minutes in the coffee shop,and enjoy the rest of your day with friends.

   - Worth of 的意思是「價值約……；等同於……」跟 worthy of 的意思不同，worthy of 是「值得的」的意思，例：He is not worthy of your time. 他不值得你花時間在他身上。

2. This all stems from the fact that human beings are lousy **at** multitasking.

   - 形容詞加 at something 可用來表達做一件事的能力或擅長程度，例：She is so good at baking. 她的烘焙能力好強。

給 Soho 族的建議

試著想想看，早上醒來，煮一杯你最愛的咖啡，然後緩緩走向公寓裡那扇能夠享受美景的窗戶。你打開電腦，瀏覽一些電子郵件，打了幾篇文件，然後在電話上進行一場協商。接著你最喜愛的電視節目開始了，於是你開始看電視，迅速地完成了幾樣工作，並在粗略地瀏覽電子郵件後，緩緩走到樓下某個有意思的地方吃午餐，順便計畫下午的工作。有時候你會帶著手提電腦，坐在咖啡店裡用四十五分鐘完成在辦公室要花五小時才能做完的工作，並和朋友一起享受其餘的時間。許多人相信這是一個在家工作者生活中典型的一天。但是，當他們真的試著在家工作，他們很快會發現他們的觀念必須與事實做一番調適。在家工作多半呈現雜亂無章的凌亂狀態：想把家事做好、收不完的電子郵件和接不完的電話，還有只會不斷增加的一堆工作和完成到一半的案子。與其說是在家工作，倒不如說家變成了工作，而你永遠無法下班離開！問題不在於工作的量，而是要找出做事的時間，還要維持家庭運作。這一切都源於一個事實—人類只要一次處理很多事情，就會變成無頭蒼蠅。所以如果你是在家工作的人，聽聽看以下的建議：盡量將工作與家庭分開。安排一個時間可以專心工作，並安排另一個不同的、用來享受舒適的家庭生活。在家裡挪出一個「辦公室」來也是很有幫助的，不管多小都可以。選定一個正式的辦公椅和辦公桌。當你需要工作時，就到那兒去工作；想要休息時，就到屋子的其他地方。從本質上說，讓你的生活盡可能單一任務化。當你在工作時，就百分之百的工作；不工作時，就也百分之百的在家裡好好放鬆。如果卡在中間，那麼結果就會是不佳的工作以及令人沮喪的家庭生活。

16

The Purpose of Law

Law as we know it exists for two purposes. It protects the rights of individuals, and it protects the property of individuals and companies. In the modern materialistic world, too many people disregard the second of these statutes. While everyone is quick to run to the court when some deed against other person is committed, many don't feel they need to pay back borrowed money, help out with their share of expenses, or not take things they don't own from others. Strangely, when questioning such people, they don't feel anything they're doing is illegal, and often take offence when it is mentioned. Watching TV, We might find time and again legal shows have two people fighting over who owes what to whom. Each time the courts decide, and that decision is what has to be obeyed. Most of us watching those shows might find them a little juvenile, for to us it seems so obvious who the guilty party is. Yet, if it was so obvious to everyone, why would people take things to court? Clearly, the law as regards to property and money is not a natural thing to understand. Unlike what TV might portray, the modern court house is not filled with murder trials and celebrity divorces. Most of what the courts confine themselves to is disputes between individuals and companies that are owed money. Sadly, most of the time there is no need even for a full trial. The attorney for the prosecutor needs to only attach a copy of the agreement and balance owed by the accused. If the defendant is lucky, there will be no sentence or time in jail. However, they can not disregard the enforcement. If they do, their luck will run out, and the rulings of the court allow the prosecutor to seize the assets of the defendant or even place a criminal charge against them.

___ 01. Which one of the two purposes mentioned above is often disregarded by too many people in the modern materialistic world?
(A) protecting the rights of individuals
(B) protecting the property of the rich
(C) protecting the property of individuals and companies
(D) protecting the rights of the poor

___ 02. Time and again _____ always have two people fighting over who owes what to whom on the TV.
(A) legal shows   (B) game shows
(C) sports shows   (D) variety shows

___ 03. What kind of things that are possibly taken to court?
(A) about individuals
(B) about property and money
(C) about personal relationship
(D) about friendship

___ 04. _____ the modern courts confine themselves to the disputes between individuals and companies that are owed money.
(A) Only a few   (B) Many   (C) None of   (D) Most of

___ 05. If the defendant disregards the _____, the assets of him / her might be seized.
(A) enforcement   (B) judge   (C) attorney   (D) plaintiff

解題技巧

抓頭

1. **抓主題句** 掌握主題句最快的方式就是抓主詞跟動詞,可以很粗略的知道這篇文章的方向為何。

↳ 主題句:

> <u>Law</u> as we know it <u>exists</u> for two purposes.

▼ 關鍵字:

① 主詞:Law　② 動詞:exists

在這篇文章中,從主題句可以掌握的是法律的存在。

▼ 其他資訊:two purposes

two purposes 是補充說明主詞法律存在有兩個目的。

抓尾

2. **抓末段重點** 了解第一段後快速掃描最後一段,因為最後一段是結尾,看完最後一段的主題句就可以粗略了解文章的走向。

↳ 主題句:

> Most of what the courts confine themselves to is disputes between individuals and companies that are <u>owed money</u>.

▼ 關鍵字:**owed money**

文章末段提到法院所審理的案件中,大多是個人與公司被拖欠資金的爭端,同樣可看出文章在討論法律的目的和處理的案件。

補強

3. **抓各段的主題句:**

↳ 主題句:

> Each time <u>the courts</u> decide, and that decision is what has to be obeyed.

▼ 關鍵字：the courts

這裡提到法院，可見主題和法律有關。

 解析

01. **(C)**　第一題問哪個選項是最不受人們重視的，文章中寫道 It protects the rights of individuals, <u>and it protects the property of individuals and companies.</u> In the modern materialistic world, too many people <u>disregard the second</u> of these statutes 許多人忽略第二點，所以答案是 (C) protecting the property of individuals and companies。

02. **(A)**　文章中寫道 Watching TV, <u>time and again legal shows have two people fighting over who owes what to whom.</u> 因此，答案是 (A) legal shows。

03. **(B)**　第三題問什麼事有可能會上法庭，文章中不斷提到財產和金錢糾紛，所以答案是 (B) about property and money。

04. **(D)**　文章中寫道 Most of what the courts confine themselves to isdisputes between individuals and companies that are owed money.，答案是 (D) Most of。

05. **(A)**　文章中寫道 However, they can not <u>disregard the enforcement. If they do,</u> their luck will run out, and the rulings of the court allow the prosecutor to <u>seize the assets of the defendant</u> or even place a criminal charge against them.，若對法律的執行置之不理，原告可以凍結被告的資產，因此，答案是 (A) enforcement。

必學詞彙

» **materialistic**
   `adj.` 唯物論的；實利主義的

» **disregard**
   `n.` 忽視；漠視；不尊重

» **mention** `v.` 提到；說起

» **enforcement**
   `n.` 實施，執行；強制；強迫

» **criminal**
   `adj.` 犯罪的；犯法的

» **jail** `n.` 監獄；拘留所

» **dispute** `n.` 爭論；爭執

文法觀念

1. Unlike what TV **might** portray, the modern court house is not filled with murder trials and celebrity divorces.

   • Might 屬於情態助動詞，帶有遲疑、婉轉的口氣，例：She might be upset over the breakup, but I'm not entirely sure. 她可能為了分手的事難過，但我也不是完全確定。

2. If they do, their luck will run out, and the rulings of the court allow the prosecutor to seize the assets of the defendant or even place a criminal charge **against** them.

   • Against 是介系詞，有「反對；與……相反」的意思，例：She is very much against the conservative ideas. 她很反對保守派的思想。也經常用在刑事事件上，例如：文章中的句子，或是 He currently has six charges against him. 他目前以六項罪名遭起訴。

法律的目的

　　我們知道法律的存在有兩個目的：保護個人的權利，以及保護個人及公司的財產。在現在這個物質的世界中，太多人忽視第二點。雖然每個做出不利他人行為的人都會很快到法院報到，但是他們之中有很多人認為自己沒必要償還借款、不必出自己該出的錢，或是不用避免拿不屬於自己的東西。奇怪的是，當你質問這樣的人時，他們並不認為自己做的事情有違法之處，而且常常在別人提起時，採取防禦的態度。看電視時，法律節目經常都是兩個人在爭奪誰欠誰什麼東西。每次都要靠法院來裁定，而該裁定就必須遵行。大多數人在收看這些節目時，可能會發現他們有點不成熟，因為對我們來說，哪一方有罪看來相當明顯，而如果對每個人來說都如此明顯，那為何人們還要找法院呢？顯然，當法律關乎財產和金錢之時，就不是件理所當然的事了。不同於電視所描繪的，現代的法院並沒有塞滿謀殺審判和名人離婚的案件。法院所審理的案件中，大部分也都是個人與公司被拖欠資金的爭端。可悲的是，很多時候根本沒必要充分審判。原告的律師只需要附上一份協議和被告所欠的金額就行了。如果被告是幸運的，將不會被判刑或是坐牢。但是他們不能將法律的執行置之不理，否則他們就沒那麼好運了，法院的裁決讓原告可以凍結被告的資產，甚至對他們提出刑事控訴。

17

The Short Cut of Travel

Traveling in the world today is geared towards the young and fit. Planes are built to accommodate as many people as possible, so the seats separated by narrow aisles are often cramped. Airports are big and crowded with hurrying people. Check-in counters are often difficult to find. Many airports have more than one terminal and travelers have to cover a long distance going from one terminal to another. So what can you do to make your journey easier if you are old and frail? When you buy your ticket, request your travel agent to arrange assistance and specify that you want a wheelchair-remember, airports are very huge that you will have to walk around to find the check-in counter. Once you reach the check-in counter, you will discover that things become much easier. Riding comfortably in a wheelchair, you will be taken to the boarding area and assisted aboard the plane. Make sure you organize your packing so that you have no cabin luggage except a small bag to keep with you in your seat. When the plane lands, you will be asked to wait in your seat until an airport official comes to provide assistance. You will then be wheeled to wherever you need to go. If you have a connecting flight, you will be taken to a special waiting area where you can rest. There will be a notice board showing details of all outgoing flights, which assistants you obtain any information you may need. When it is time to board your fight, an attendant will deliver you to the boarding area by wheelchair and you will be assisted onto the plane. On arrival at your final destination, you will be assisted in collecting yourluggage. There will be no delay at immigration or customs, as you will be wheeled to the check points reserved for the crew. The attendant will accompany you, with your luggage, all the way to the arrivals hall.

___ 01. Traveling in the world today is geared towards_____.
    (A) the short and weak   (B) the old and frail
    (C) the young and fit   (D) the disabled and frail

___ 02. According to the passage, which sentence is not right?
    (A) The seats in the plane are usually separated by narrow aisles.
    (B) Airports are huge and crowded and the check-in counter is not easy to find.
    (C) In fact, many airports have more than one terminal.
    (D) There is a short distance between two terminals.

___ 03. Who can the old and frail ask for assistance when they buy tickets?
    (A) the stewardess   (B) the travel agent
    (C) the airport official   (D) the attendant

___ 04. According to the article, when you reach_____, things will become much easier.
    (A) the check-in counter   (B) the terminal
    (C) the aisle   (D) the arrivals hall

___ 05. According to the passage, which sentence is wrong?
    (A) You will be required to wait until an airport official comes when the plane lands.
    (B) If you have a connecting flight, you will have to wait in a special area.
    (C) There might be some delay at immigration or customs.
    (D) The attendant will accompany you to the arrivals hall.

解題技巧

1. **抓主題句** 掌握主題句最快的方式就是抓主詞跟動詞,可以
很粗略的知道這篇文章的方向為何。

↳ 主題句:

> Traveling in the world today is geared towards the young and fit.

▼ 關鍵字:

① 主詞:Traveling　② 動詞:geared towards
在這篇文章中,從主題句可以掌握的是旅行和適合的對象。

▼ 其他資訊:

the young and fit 是補充説明旅行適合的對象是年輕健康的人。

抓頭

2. **抓末段重點** 了解第一段後快速掃描最後一段,因為最後
一段是結尾,看完最後一段的主題句就可以
粗略了解文章的走向。

↳ 主題句:

> On arrival at your final destination, you will be assisted in collecting your luggage.

▼ 關鍵字:final destination
文章末段在説明抵達目的地的情況。

抓尾

3. **抓各段的主題句**：

↳ 主題句：

> So what can you do to make your journey easier if you are old and frail?

▼ 關鍵字：old and frail

這裡提出問題，老弱者能如何讓旅途變得更輕鬆？同樣能看出文章在討論旅行。

 解析

01. **(C)** 文章的主題句寫道 Traveling in the world today is geared towards the young and fit.，答案是 (C) the young and fit。

02. **(D)** 第二題問下列何者是錯的，文章中提到航廈之間的距離很遙遠，所以答案 (D) There is a short distance between two terminals. 為錯誤。

03. **(B)** 第三題問老弱者訂機票時可以請誰幫忙安排協助，文章中寫道 When you buy your ticket, request your travel agent to arrange assistance and specify that you want a wheelchair，因此答案是 (B) the travel agent。

04. **(A)** 文章中寫道 Once you reach the check-in counter, you will discover that things become much easier. 答案是 (A) the check-in counter。

05. **(C)** 第五題問下列何者是錯的，文章中提到 There will be no delay at immigration or customs, 不會被耽擱在入境處或海關，因此答案 (C) There might be somedelay at immigration or customs. 是錯的。

 **必學詞彙**

> » **accommodate**
>   **v.** 能容納
>
> » **narrow**
>   **adj.** 狹小的，狹窄的
>
> » **assistance**
>   **n.** 援助；幫助
>
> » **immigration**
>   **n.** 移居；移民
>
> » **luggage** **n.** 行李
>
> » **specific**
>   **adj.** 明確的；具體的
>
> » **separated** **adj.** 分居的

 文法觀念

1. <u>Many airports have more than one terminal and travelers have to cover a long distance going **from one terminal to another**.</u>

   • From one to another 是常見的用法，another 是沒有限定範圍的，意思是「另一個」但沒有特定指哪一個，例：I need another box. 我需要另一個箱子。（用 another 代表很多個箱子裡的其中任一個）。

2. <u>When it is time to board your flight, an attendant will deliver you to the boarding area by wheelchair and you will be assisted **onto** the plane.</u>

   • Onto 是「到……之上」的意思，跟 on 有時可通用，有時則不可，例如：本句的 onto 若換成 on 就變成了「服務員會在飛機上協助你」而不是「服務員會協助你登機」，可通用的情形像是「某人上去某個地方」例：He climbed on/onto the tree like a monkey. 他像隻猴子般爬到樹上。或 I went on/onto the plane. 我上了飛機。

旅行的捷徑

今日的世界旅遊較適合年輕人和健康的人。飛機的建造以盡可能容納最多人為主，狹小的座位以一條小走道分隔開來。機場大又充滿了匆忙的人。登機櫃檯往往難以找到。許多機場有多個航空站，而且從一個航站到另一個航站，需要很長的距離。因此，如果您是年長人士，您可以做什麼，讓您的旅途更容易？在您購買機票時，要求旅行社安排支援，並具體說明您要一張輪椅，要記得，機場是非常大的，您得繞來繞去才能找到報到櫃檯。但只要您到達櫃檯，就會發現事情容易多了。您會舒舒服服地坐在輪椅上，被帶往登機處，並會有人協助您登機。請確實整理好您的行李，這樣一來，您除了一個隨身放在座位上的小提包之外，就不用另外帶著登機箱了。當飛機降落時，您會被要求在座位上等待，直到機場職員過來提供協助。您將會坐著輪椅被帶至任何您需要去的地方。如果您需要轉機，就會被帶到一個特定的等候區休息。那裡會有告示板，列出所有離境班機的詳細資料，而且協助您的人會幫您取得任何可能需要的資料。到了該登機時，服務人員會用輪椅把您送到登機區並協助您登機。在抵達的最終目的地後，也會有人幫您領取行李。而且也不會被耽擱在入境處或海關，因為您會被推到為機組人員服務的檢查站。服務人員會陪著您，帶著您的行李，一路直達入境大廳。

18

How does Stress Influence Our Health

Most people might think of stress as just a mental thing - unmanageable pressures, worries and anxieties of modern life. In fact, these are just some of the common causes of stress. Stress is a natural human reaction; it is the body's instinct response to problems. It is a physical malfunction of handling problems. Stress creates a variety of problems in our lives. When we are stressed, we can feel our muscles are stiff, our brains are shattered, and our tempers are short. These can go from short-term anxiety to long-term health problems. It drains our energy and strength to face problems and it affects our lives in many ways. The depression and frustration caused by stress can spill over into every area of our lives; further, they damage our hard earned success and limit opportunities for achievement. Because stress can be such a destructive force but something that we can't avoid, here are some simple steps suggested by experts that can help to relieve the stress. One of the best way to alleviate stress is to list of all the issues and problems that are causing you stress. Split the list into two sections, "Trivial" and "Serious". Make sure that you write down everything. The process of writing your problems down will help you see them in a different way and have a clear mind. After writing down problems, browse through the list, and focus on the smaller issues that often cause more stress first. Make it a priority to solve these small issues because usually they are within your control. Having fixed all the petty problems will gain you more confidence and improve your concentration. Thus, you are given a better starting point to overcome the bigger issues in your life. Try to be more flexible, look at problems from different angles, stop grasping onto the stresses that you can't control over, and try solving the stresses that you do have control over. At the end, if you still find that the anxiety and depression is uncontrollable, seek for help from physicians or professional organizations.

___ 01. Which of the following factors was not mentioned as the cause of stresses in the article?
(A) unmanageable pressures   (B) anxieties of modern life
(C) worries   (D) bad living conditions

___ 02. When we are _____, we can feel our muscles are stiff, our brains are shattered, and our tempers are short.
(A) stressed   (B) happy   (C) nervous   (D) frightened

___ 03. Referring to the text, one of the best ways to alleviate stress is to _____ .
(A) do exercises   (B) eat food
(C) list "Trivial" and "Serious" issues   (D) shout loudly

___ 04. After writing down problems, people should solve the _____ first.
(A) big problems   (B) small issues
(C) important issues   (D) difficult problems

___ 05. If you still find that the stress is uncontrollable, you'd better seek for help from _____ .
(A) professional organizations   (B) parents
(C) policeman   (D) lawyer

解題技巧 ————————————————

抓
頭

1. **抓主題句** 掌握主題句最快的方式就是抓主詞跟動詞，可以很粗略的知道這篇文章的方向為何。

↳ 主題句：

> Most people might think of stress as just a mental thing - unmanageable pressures, worries and anxieties of modern life.

▼ 關鍵字：

① 主詞：Most people　② 動詞：think of stress

在這篇文章中，從主題句可以掌握的是大多數人對於壓力的想法。

▼ 其他資訊：a mental thing

是補充說明大多數人只認為壓力是跟精神有關的事。

抓
尾

2. **抓末段重點** 了解第一段後快速掃描最後一段，因為最後一段是結尾，看完最後一段的主題句就可以粗略了解文章的走向。

↳ 主題句：

> At the end, if you still find that the anxiety and depression is uncontrollable, seek for help from physicians or professional organizations.

▼ 關鍵字：the anxiety and depression

文章末段提到若仍覺得焦慮和抑鬱無法控制，必須去尋求專業協助。

3. 抓各段的主題句：

↳ 主題句：

> The process of writing your problems down will help you see them in a different way and have a clear mind.

▼ 關鍵字：a clear mind

這在講把問題寫下來能幫助釐清思緒，能看出文章在討論解決心中的問題，也就是煩惱和壓力。

 解析

01. **(D)** 第一題問的是壓力的成因，文章並未提及居住環境，所以答案是 (D) bad living conditions。

02. **(A)** 文章中寫道 When we are stressed, we can feel our muscles are stiff, our brains are shattered, and our tempers are short. ，所以答案是 (A) stressed。

03. **(C)** 第三題問舒緩壓力最好的方式，文章說寫下問題最有幫助，所以答案是 (C) list "Trivial" and "Serious" issues。

04. **(B)** 第四題問寫下問題後，我們該先解決哪些問題，文章說要優先解決能掌控的小問題，答案是 (B) small issues。

05. **(A)** 第五題問若仍覺得焦慮和抑鬱無法控制，要去尋求誰的幫助，文章中寫道 "At the end, if you still find that the anxiety and depression is uncontrollable, seek for help from physicians or professional organizations."，因此，答案是 (A) professional organizations。

 **必學詞彙**

> **unmanageable**
> [adj.] 難操縱的；難控制的

> **concentration**
> [n.] 專心；專注

> **professional**
> [adj.] 職業性的；專業的

> **flexible** [adj.] 柔韌的；有彈性的

> **uncontrollable**
> [adj.] 控制不住的；無法管束的

> **improve** [v.] 改進；改善

> **variety**
> [n.] 多樣化；多變化

 文法觀念

1. It drains our energy and strength to face problems and it affects our lives **in many ways**.

 - In many ways 是「以很多方式」的意思，中間的單字可以替換，例：in a lot of ways 也是指「以很多方式」、in several ways 以幾個方式，或是單數的 in a way,... 以一種方式，這幾種説法都能用來表達對某一件事情的影響廣泛程度。

2. Make it a priority to solve these small issues because usually they are **within** your control.

 - Within 屬於限定詞，意思是「在……之內」，可以用來限定時間或範圍，例：Within seconds, the lion shredded the buffalo to pieces. 幾秒之間，獅子便把水牛碎屍萬段。

 **中文翻譯**

壓力對健康的影響

　　大多數人可能覺得壓力只不過跟精神有關，就是那些現代生活中無法控制的壓力、擔憂和焦慮。事實上，這些只是壓力的常見因素。壓力是一種自然的人類反應；它是身體遇到問題時本能的反應。它是處理問題時發生的身體機能失常。壓力會在我們生活中製造各種問題。當我們感受到壓力時，我們會感覺到肌肉僵硬、精神耗弱以及脾氣暴躁。這些會從造成短期焦慮一直到引發長期的健康問題。它不僅耗盡我們面對問題的能量和力氣，也在很多方面影響我們的生活。壓力造成的抑鬱和沮喪，會波及到我們生活中的每一個領域，它們會進一步地破壞我們得之不易的成功，並限制實現抱負的機會。因為壓力是如此無法避免的毀滅性力量，這裡有一些專家建議的簡單步驟，可以幫助減輕壓力。要減輕壓力，其中一個最好的方式，是將所有造成壓力的事件和問題列出來。將名單分為兩部分──「普通」和「嚴重」。一定要把每件事都寫下來。寫的過程會幫助你以不同的角度看待這些問題，並且有個清晰的頭腦。在寫下問題之後，把清單瀏覽一遍，然後先將注意力集中在造成較多壓力的小問題上。優先解決這些小問題，因為通常它們是你可以掌握的。搞定那些瑣碎小問題，不僅會讓你更有自信，同時也會改善你的專注力。如此一來，你就有了一個較好的起點，可以去解決你生活中更大的問題。試著有彈性一點，用不同的角度看待問題，不要一直抓著你無法控制的壓力不放，並解決那些你可以控制的壓力。最後，如果你仍然覺得焦慮和抑鬱是你無法控制的，就尋求精神科醫生或專業組織的協助吧。

19

A Manager's Responsibility

During the period of economic recession, millions of people have been thrown into unemployment. However, the employees who manage to survive from the worldwide layoff may suffer from insecurity and negative thoughts which will damage the team spirit of a corporation in the long run. Thus, the most serious work a manager can do to reestablish a team environment is to work on the leadership skills. While a manager manages the present situation, a leader leads the team into the future. A key part of that leadership is the willingness to innovate. A true leader motivates a team by asking questions, and poking at current policy to see if something better can be found. In short, it's the willingness to be open to excellence and change as well as to involve each team member in those efforts that motivates a team. When a team is suddenly reorganized due to the economic difficulty, many supervisors fail to see the strengths and weaknesses of each team member. To a great extent, leadership resembles the role a coach plays on a sports team. A good coach knows the players well enough so each of them can be put in a role that will maximize that person's usefulness. Like a good coach, a true leader should be constantly aware of whether each team member is being challenged and willing to grow in his or her areas of weakness to enhance the team. Even though team building can't be a short-term job, it's still possible to have some fun. Office parties can be great motivators as they help team members get to know each other in a relaxing environment. Many team members don't trust each other simply because they don't know each other. Parties provide opportunities for conversations which help a team to form bonds. The keystones of building a good team are trust, communication, and involvement; it's a part of a manager's everyday work to provide innovation and know how to use the strengths of the team to best advantage.

___ 01. _____ threw millions of people into unemployment.
(A) Economic recession　(B) The earthquake
(C) World war　(D) Economic prosperity

___ 02. According to the second paragraph, the key part of the leadership is _____.
(A) the creativity　(B) the scope of innovation
(C) the power to innovate　(D) willingness to innovate

___ 03. _____ can be great motivators to help team members get to know each other in a relaxing environment.
(A) Having a meeting　(B) Office parties
(C) Working together　(D) Chatting

___ 04. To a great extent, leadership resembles the role of a _____ on a sports team.
(A) teacher　(B) player　(C) coach　(D) manager

解題技巧 ─────────────────

1. **抓主題句** 掌握主題句最快的方式就是抓主詞跟動詞,可以
   很粗略的知道這篇文章的方向為何。

   ↳ 主題句:

   > Thus, the most serious work <u>a manager</u> can <u>do</u> to
   > reestablish a team environment is to work on the leadership
   > skills.

   ▼ 關鍵字:

   ① 主詞:a manager　　② 動詞:do
   在這篇文章中,從主題句可以掌握的是經理人和做事。

   ▼ 其他資訊:

   the most serious work 是補充說明主詞 a manager 要做的
   事。

2. **抓末段重點** 了解第一段後快速掃描最後一段,因為最後
   一段是結尾,看完最後一段的主題句就可以
   粗略了解文章的走向。

   ↳ 主題句:

   > The keystones of building a good team are trust,
   > communication and involvement; it's a part of <u>a manager's</u>
   > <u>everyday work</u> to provide innovation and know how to use the
   > strengths of the team to best advantage.

   ▼ 關鍵字:a manager's everyday work
   文章末段提到管理者的職責。

抓
頭

抓
尾

226

3. 抓各段的主題句：

↳ 主題句：

> To a great extent, <u>leadership</u> resembles the role a coach plays on a sports team.

▼ 關鍵字：leadership

這裡在討論領導階層，同樣能看出文章在講管理和領導的學問。

解析

01. **(A)** 文章中寫道 During the period of <u>economic recession</u>, millions of people have been thrown into unemployment.，答案是 (A) Economic recession。

02. **(D)** 文章中寫道 A key part of that leadership is <u>the willingness to innovate.</u>，答案是 (D) willingness to innovate。

03. **(B)** 文章中寫道 <u>Office parties</u> can be great motivators as they help team members get to know each other in a relaxing environment.，答案是 (B) Office parties。

04. **(C)** 文章中寫道 To a great extent, leadership resembles the role a coach plays on a sports team.，答案是 (C) coach。

必學詞彙

» **recession**
　n. 後退；退回

» **corporation**
　n. 法人；股份（有限）
　　公司

» **reestablish**
　v. 重建；重新設立

» **willingness** **n.** 自願；樂意

» **weakness**
　n. 弱點；缺點

» **motivator**
　n. 激發因素；（行為）
　　動力

» **involvement** **n.** 參與

文法觀念

1. A true leader motivates a team by asking questions, and poking at current policy to see **if** something better can be found.

   • If 在此不解釋為「如果」，而是「是否……」的意思，例：I'm not sure if he likes me or not. 我不確定他是否喜歡我。

2. To a great extent, leadership resembles the role a coach plays on a sports team.

   • On 通常是「在上方」的意思，在本句中，on 則用來説明一支隊伍的情況，例：She is the best player on our team. 她是我們隊上最厲害的選手。

中文翻譯 ─────────────────────────

經理人的責任

在經濟衰退期間，數百萬的人被迫失業。然而，那些想辦法要在這波全球性的裁員潮中生存下來的員工，長期下來可能會因為沒有安全感以及負面思維而破壞一個公司的團隊精神。因此，一個經理人對重建團隊環境所能做的最認真的事就是好好培養其領導能力。一個經理人是在管理現狀，而一個領導者卻是帶領著團隊迎向未來。領導力的關鍵部分在於改革的意願。一個真正的領袖會透過提問、檢視目前的政策來看看能不能發現更好的東西來激勵團隊。簡言之，要激勵一個團隊，就是願意對卓越與變化抱持開放態度，並讓每個團隊成員都一起努力。當一個團隊突然因為經濟困境而面臨被重組的命運時，許多主管看不出每個團隊成員的優勢和弱勢。在很大程度上，領導階層人員的角色就像是一支運動隊伍的教練。一個好的教練會對他的選手瞭若指掌，知道他們每一個人在哪一個位置能發揮最大的用處。就像一個優秀的教練一樣，一個真正的領導人應該不斷地去了解每個團隊成員是否受到挑戰仍願意在其不足之處有所長進，以提升團隊能力。即使團隊建設不是短期的工作，它仍可能有一些樂趣。辦公室派對就是絕妙的激勵方式，能幫助團隊成員在輕鬆的環境中對彼此更加了解。許多團隊成員彼此不信任，就是因為對彼此認識得不夠多。派對讓他們有機會可以說說話，有助於聯繫團隊。建立一個好團隊之基石在於信任、溝通及參與。一個管理者工作的一部分，就是要改革以及知道如何使用團隊的強項來取得最佳優勢。

20

The "Shanzhai" Effect

Today, "Shanzhai" is undoubtedly the most heated term that originated from the internet in China. The term "Shanzhai" was used to indicate a copycat cellphone at first, and now it's a label for any fake products and all low-cost, profit-oriented imitation cultural activities. Actually, a variety of Shanzhai products which are made to suit peasants who account for most of the Chinese population has evolved into the "Shanzhai" phenomenon or even the "Shanzhai" culture. Western media described the Shanzhai phenomenon and presented it as a form of rebellion and resistance to the society and the mainstream culture. Shanzhai products are being very popular because they are not only multi-function but also cheap. To most consumers, low price is the key. Take a Shanzhai iPhone for example; it costs only a bit more than one thousand RMB while an original one costs at least four thousand RMB or more. Pursuing low costs, nearly all trades and professions in China are consequently Shanzhai-oriented, from outfits, super stars, TV shows to authoritative events. Not too long ago, a Shanzhai iPod advertisement used a Shanzhai singer to promote its Shanzhai products; meanwhile, a famous actress attended a formal fashion ceremony in a Shanzhai designer's dressing gown, which provoked much discussion. According to an investigation into Shanzhai culture on the Internet, over seventy percent of people think that Shanzhai culture is merely a duplicate culture or an imitation culture while only about thirty percent of people believe that it is basically a piracy. The Shanzhai phenomenon also draws the attention of the whole world, for this copycat culture not only hampers genuine creativity and invades property rights, but also influences the global economy tremendously. Some do advocate establishing relevant legislation that will eliminate the "Shanzhai" phenomenon. Nevertheless, there are still more than forty percent of people highly approve such subculture. Some experts in China even claimed that Shanzhai culture shows the great grass-root power of Chinese people.

___ 01. Which sentence is not true about "Shanzhai" ?
    (A) It is a term originated from the Internet in China.
    (B) It was used to indicate a copycat cell phone at first.
    (C) Now it's a label for any fake products.
    (D) Western media thought highly of it.

___ 02. Shanzhai products are being very popular mainly because they are _____.
    (A) expensive   (B) very cheap
    (C) quite beautiful   (D) made of advanced technology

___ 03. You are possible to buy a Shanzhai iPhone at _____.
    (A) less than one thousand RMB
    (B) a bit more than one thousand RMB
    (C) at least four thousand RMB
    (D) at most four thousand RMB

___ 04. According to an investigation, about _____ of people believe that it is basically a piracy.
    (A) 70%   (B) 60%   (C) 40%   (D) 30%

___ 05. Which sentence is wrong about the copycat culture?
   (A) It hampers genuine creativity.
   (B) It invades property rights.
   (C) It influences the global economy greatly.
   (D) It is highly approved by most people.

 解題技巧 ────────────────

抓頭

1. **抓主題句** 掌握主題句最快的方式就是抓主詞跟動詞，可以
   很粗略的知道這篇文章的方向為何。
   ↳ 主題句：

   > Today, "Shanzhai" is undoubtedly the most heated term
   > that originated from the Internet in China.

   ▼ 關鍵字：
   ① 主詞： "Shanzhai"   ② 動詞：is
   在這篇文章中，從主題句可以掌握的是山寨一詞。

   ▼ 其他資訊：
   originated from the Internet in China. 是補充說明主詞
   "Shanzhai" 的起源。

抓尾

2. **抓末段重點** 了解第一段後快速掃描最後一段，因為最後
   一段是結尾，看完最後一段的主題句就可以
   粗略了解文章的走向。
   ↳ 主題句：

   > Some experts in China even claimed that Shanzhai culture
   > shows the great grass-root power of Chinese people.

   ▼ 關鍵字：Shanzhai culture
   文章末段提到中國專家對於山寨文化的主張。

3. 抓各段的主題句：

↳ 主題句：

> Shanzhai products are being very <u>popular</u> because they are not only multi-function but also cheap.

▼ 關鍵字：popular

這在講山寨商品流行的原因，同樣能看出文章在討論山寨文化。

解析

01. **(D)** 第一題問下列何者為誤，文中提及西方媒體對於山寨的評價為 "a form of rebellion and resistance to the society and the mainstream culutre."，因此，答案是 (D) Western media thought highly of it.。

02. **(B)** 第二題問山寨商品流行的原因，文中提到原因是多功能且便宜，符合的選項是 (B) very cheap。

03. **(B)** 文章中寫道 Take a Shanzhai iPhone for example; it costs only <u>a bit more than one thousand RMB</u> while an original one costs at least four thousand RMB or more.，所以答案是 (B) a bit more than one thousand RMB。

04. **(D)** 第四題問調查中有多少人認為山寨是剽竊行為，文中寫道 while only about <u>thirty percent</u> of people believe that it is basically a piracy. 所以答案是 (D) 30%。

05. **(D)** 第五題問下列何者為誤，文章最後一段寫道 Nevertheless, there are still <u>more than forty percent of people highly approve such subculture.</u> 超過百分之四十不算大多數人，因此，答案是 (D) It is highly approve by most people.。

 **必學詞彙**

> **undoubtedly**
> adv. 毫無疑問地；肯定地
>
> **imitation**
> n. 模仿；模擬；仿造
>
> **rebellion**
> n. 反叛；造反；叛亂
>
> **duplicate**
> adj. 錯誤；過失

> **phenomenon**
> n. 現象；稀有的事；奇蹟
>
> **eliminate**
> v. 排除；消除
>
> **authoritative**
> adj. 權威性的；官方的

 文法觀念

1. <u>Not too long ago, a Shanzhai iPod advertisement used a Shanzhai singer to promote its Shanzhai products;</u> **meanwhile**, <u>a famous actress attended a formal fashion ceremony in a Shanzhai designer's dressing gown, which provoked much discussion.</u>

- Meanwhile 是副詞，有連接作用，meanwhile 的意思是「同時」，通常用來連接兩件有關連的事情，例：He is working in the coal mine; meanwhile, she is at home taking care of kids. 他在礦坑工作，同時，她在家裡帶小孩。

2. <u>Nevertheless, there are still more than forty percent of people</u>
   <u>highly approve **such** subculture.</u>

   • Such 在本句中是「這樣的、如此的」的意思，在文章中用
     來說明前方提到的事物，例：We definitely would not
     condone such violence. 我們絕不允許這樣的暴力。

 中文翻譯 ─────────────────────────

山寨效應

　　今日，源於網路的「山寨」一詞，無疑是中國最夯的名詞。
「山寨」這個詞，一開始被用來指稱仿冒手機，現在成了所有
仿冒產品和低成本、利潤取向的模仿文化活動的標籤。事實上，
各式各樣為了迎合中國大部分人口的市井小民所製造的山寨產
品，已經發展出「山寨現象」，甚至是「山寨文化」了。西方
媒體形容並介紹這個山寨現象為對社會體制和主流文化的一種
反叛和抵制。「山寨」產品因多功能又便宜而非常受歡迎。對
大部分消費者來說，低價就是關鍵。以山寨 iPhone 為例，它
只要一千多元人民幣，而原版的至少要四千多塊。因為追求低
成本，中國幾乎各行各業都走「山寨」潮，從服裝、明星、電
視劇到官方活動都有「山寨」版。不久之前，一款「山寨版」
iPod 廣告用一名「山寨版」歌手來推銷其山寨產品；於此同時，
一個著名的女演員穿著一席「山寨版」設計師禮服出席正式時
尚典禮，引發了諸多議論。一項就「山寨文化」進行的調查顯
示，超過百分之七十的人認為山寨文化不過就是一種複製文化
或仿冒文化；僅有百分之三十的人認為山寨文化說穿了就是一

種剽竊行為。山寨現象同時引起了全世界的關注，因為這冒牌文化不僅抑制了真正的創意、侵犯了產權，同時也影響世界經濟甚鉅。的確有人提倡設立相關法律以消滅山寨現象；然而，仍然有超過百分之四十以上的人高度贊同這樣的次文化。有些中國專家甚至主張「山寨文化展現了中國人民了不起的草根力量。」

21

Social Activities at Work

Most people make friends at school, via hobbies or through a family or friends' connection. Other than these common avenues for making friends, we also make new friends at work. For not quite a few people, their jobs are more than just the work that goes from 9 a.m. to 5 p.m. every day, but an important socializing activity. People who work in the same office usually have the same educational background and often share related assignments that make they associate with their colleagues naturally. Some generous supervisors can be enthusiastic enough to hold social get-togethers frequently in their own houses or at wherever suitable. The social get-together can be a picnic or a dinner party. Some employers will invite their subordinates to visit his home. It is a good chance for them to have more interaction with each other outside their offices. They will be introduced to other guests and family members, and then chat or play cards in groups. The host will have drinks or refreshments available for everyone who comes to their home. People could come and leave during the hours. Generally, subordinates don't refuse such social gatherings unless they have something much more important to do. Besides private gatherings, many corporations hold at least one major activity every year, such as a big feast during Christmastime or a yearly banquet in celebration of the New Year. Lots of big companies also have annual sports meets or company outings where employees and administrators can play sports or have fun together. More and more employers or administrators realize the importance of business social potential and will try their best to build a family atmosphere on the job so that the employees will feel cozy and secure in the working environment, which is beneficial for not only the employees themselves and their family, but also the company and the whole society.

___ 01. From the first paragraph, people can make friends _____.
    (A) at school   (B) at work
    (C) through friends' connection   (D) all of the above

___ 02. From the passage, we can infer that most people work
    _____.
    (A) from 9 a.m. to 5 p.m   (B) from 8 a.m. to 6 p.m
    (C) from 8:30 a.m. to 5 p.m   (D) from 9 a.m. to 6 p.m

___ 03. Usually, the subordinates _____ social gatherings unless they have something more important to do.
    (A) can refuse   (B) don't refuse
    (C) don't want to accept   (D) never accept

___ 04. More and more employers or administrators realize the importance of _____ on the job.
    (A) the working condition   (B) business social potential
    (C) the working atmosphere   (D) the leadership

___ 05. What does the text talk about?
    (A) social activities at school   (B) social activities at home
    (C) social activities at work   (D) social activities during holiday

解題技巧

抓頭

1. **抓主題句** 掌握主題句最快的方式就是抓主詞跟動詞,可以很粗略的知道這篇文章的方向為何。

↪ 主題句:

> Most people <u>make friends</u> at school, via hobbies or through a family or friends' connection.

▼ 關鍵字:

① 主詞:Most people　② 動詞:make friends
在這篇文章中,從主題句可以掌握的是關於「大多數人」和「交朋友」。

▼ 其他資訊:

via hobbies or through a family or friends' connection.
說明大多數人交朋友的方式。

抓尾

2. **抓末段重點** 了解第一段後快速掃描最後一段,因為最後一段是結尾,看完最後一段的主題句就可以粗略了解文章的走向。

↪ 主題句:

> More and more employers or administrators realize <u>the importance of business social potential</u> and will try their best to build a family atmosphere on the job so that the employees will feel cozy and secure in the working environment, which is beneficial for not only the employees themselves and their family, but also the company and the whole society.

▼ 關鍵字:the importance of business social potential
文章末段提到商務社交的潛在力量,同樣能看出文章主題是工作上的社交活動。

3. **抓各段的主題句：**
↳ 主題句：

> Some generous supervisors can be enthusiastic enough to hold <u>social get-togethers</u> frequently in their own houses or at wherever suitable.

▼ 關鍵字：social get-togethers
這裡提到有些主管會辦社交聚會。

解析

01. **(D)**　第一題問根據文章，人們能以何種方式交朋友，文章中寫道 Most people make friends <u>at school</u>, via hobbies or <u>through a family or friends' connection</u>. Other than these common avenues for making friends, we also make new friends <u>at work</u>. ，所以答案是 (D) all of the above。

02. **(A)**　第二題問根據文章，文章中寫道 For not quite a few people, their jobs are more than just the work that goes <u>from 9 a.m. to 5 p.m.</u> every day 答案是 (A) from 9 a.m. to 5 p.m。

03. **(B)**　第三題問接到邀請，部屬通常有何反應，文章中寫道 Generally, subordinates <u>don't refuse</u> such social gatherings unless they have something much more important to do. 答案是 (B) don't refuse。

04. **(B)** 文章中寫道 More and more employers or administrators realize the importance of <u>business social potential</u> and will try their best to build a family atmosphere on the job，所以答案是 (B) business social potential。

05. **(C)** 第五題問的是文章主旨，經過三個步驟之後，可看出文章在討論工作上的社交行為，所以答案是 (C) social activities at work。

 **必學詞彙**

» **connection**
n. 關係；關聯

» **avenue**
n. 大街；大道；途徑

» **socialize**
v. 參與社交；交際

» **gathering**
n. 集會；聚集

» **beneficial**
adj. 有益的；有利的

» **associate**
n. 夥伴；同事；朋友

» **enthusiastic**
adj. 熱情的；熱烈的；熱心的

 **文法觀念**

1. <u>Most people make friends at school, **via** hobbies or through a</u>
   <u>family or friends' connection.</u>

   - Via 是「藉由；經由」的意思，用來說明途徑或達到某事物
     的方式，例：I sent you a parcel via airmail. 我透過航空郵件
     寄了包裹給你。或 We will contact you via email. 我們會透過
     電子郵件聯絡你。

2. <u>**Lots of** big companies also have annual sports meets or company</u>
   <u>outings where employees and administrators can play sports orhave</u>
   <u>fun together.</u>

   - Lots of是一種口語化的說法，用來形容「大量的；很多的」，
     例：Lots of people don't know how to cook. 很多人不會煮飯。

職場社交

　　多數人在學校透過嗜好，或經由家人或朋友牽線來交朋友。除了這些常見的交友管道之外，我們也會在工作場合交新朋友。對不少人來説，他們的職業不僅是每天朝九晚五的工作，也是一個重要的社交活動。在同一個辦公室工作的人經常有相同的學術背景，而且通常分擔相關的工作任務，因此他們很自然地就會和同事為伍。有些大方的主管很熱心，經常會在他們自己家或是任何適合的地方舉辦社交聚會。這種社交聚會可以是一場野餐或是一場晚餐派對。有些老闆會邀請他們的部屬到家裡來。這對他們來説是個很好的機會，能在辦公室外的地方有更多的互動。他們會被介紹給其他的賓客和家庭成員，然後就成群地聊天或是玩牌。主人會為每個人準備飲料或點心，在聚會的這段時間人們可以自由來去。一般而言，除非有更重要的事情，否則部屬不會拒絕這類的社交聚會。除了私人聚會之外，很多企業每年會至少舉辦一次大活動，例如：聖誕期間的盛大餐會，或是慶祝新年的年終尾牙。很多大公司也有年度的運動會或是公司旅遊，讓員工及主管能運動或是一起玩。越來越多雇主或管理人體認到商務社交的潛在力量，因此都會盡可能地讓工作有家庭氣氛，如此一來，員工會對工作環境感到舒服且安全。而這不僅對員工本身以及員工的家庭有益，而且對公司以及整個社會都有好處。

22

The OCD Symptoms

For many people, David Beckham is a superstar in the football profession, and he is also known for his charming smile and fashion style. However, not many people know that Beckham has been struggling with obsessive-compulsive disorder (OCD), which is the fourth most common mental disorder. OCD may involve intrusive thoughts that produce anxiety, repetitive behaviors intended for reducing anxiety, and combinations of obsessions and compulsive behaviors. The OCD sufferers frequently perform compulsions to seek relief from obsession-related anxiety. A relative indistinct obsession could involve a sense of disorder, accompanied by an emotional threat when the imbalance remains in life. For example, many OCD sufferers have a great fear of contamination such as germs, so they repeatedly wash their hands. And those who suffer from more severe obsessions may be preoccupied with the idea of violently hurting others or themselves. Most of these sufferers do not enact or like these aggressive ideas, but are frustrated by some sexual, religious or vicious impulses, and the fact that they may inexplicably harm someone. The OCD symptoms can be alienating and time-consuming, not to mention the great emotional and economic loss. Yet, it has been accepted that behavioral therapy can be an effective treatment for OCD. The technique used in OCD behavioral therapy is called exposure and ritual prevention (ERP); this treatment involves gradually learning to be tolerant of the anxiety related to not performing the ritual behavior. For example, someone may see a few dirty spots on the floor and try to clean them with a cloth once (exposure)without coming back to double check if the floor is clean (ritual prevention). Thus the next level of this treatment will be not cleaning the dirty spots at all. Nowadays OCD is diagnosed nearly as common as asthma and diabetes. People who have OCD don't have to isolate themselves or endure the complaint alone. The treatment for OCD can be rigorous, and the patients must be motivated with strong conviction. Using ERP, a patient can be completely symptom free.

___ 01. Who is David Beckham?
    (A) a famous singer   (B) a famous football player
    (C) a famous actor   (D) a famous cook

___ 02. According to the article, _____ know that Beckham has been struggling with obsessive-compulsive disorder (OCD).
    (A) Everybody   (B) Nobody
    (C) Most of people   (D) Not many

___ 03. Which of the following is not the symptom of OCD?
    (A) fear of contamination   (B) repetitive behaviors
    (C) keep laughing   (D) wash hands again and again

___ 04. _____ has been accepted as an effective treatment for OCD.
    (A) Behavioral therapy   (B) Occupational therapy
    (C) Drug therapy   (D) Specific therapy

___ 05. Nowadays OCD is considered to be _____.
    (A) very rare   (B) as common as diabetes
    (C) can't be cured   (D) very serious

解題技巧

抓頭

1. **抓主題句** 掌握主題句最快的方式就是抓主詞跟動詞,可以很粗略的知道這篇文章的方向為何。

↳ 主題句:

> The OCD sufferers frequently perform compulsions to seek relief from obsession-related anxiety.

▼ 關鍵字:

① 主詞:OCD sufferers ② 動詞:perform

在這篇文章中,從主題句可以掌握的是 OCD 強迫症患者和做強迫性動作。

▼ 其他資訊:

compulsions 是補充說明主詞 OCD sufferers 展現出的行為。

抓尾

2. **抓末段重點** 了解第一段後快速掃描最後一段,因為最後一段是結尾,看完最後一段的主題句就可以粗略了解文章的走向。

↳ 主題句:

> The treatment for OCD can be rigorous, and the patients must be motivated with strong conviction. Using ERP, a patient can be
>
> completely symptom free.

▼ 關鍵字:treatment

文章末段提到強迫症的治療。

3. 抓各段的主題句：

↳ 主題句：

> The OCD <u>symptoms</u> can be alienating and time-consuming, not to mention the great emotional and economic loss.

▼ 關鍵字：symptoms

這裡在講強迫症的症狀，和它帶來的精神、經濟損失，同樣能看出文章的主題是強迫症。

解析

01. **(B)** 第一題問誰是 David Beckham，文章開頭提到 David Beckham is a superstar in <u>the football profession</u>，所以答案是 (B) a famous football player。

02. **(D)** 文章中寫道 However, <u>not many people</u> know that Beckham has been struggling with obsessive-compulsive disorder (OCD), which is the fourth most common mental disorder. 所以答案是 (D) Not many。

03. **(C)** 第三題問哪個選項不是強迫症的症狀，文章中提到 For example, many OCD sufferers have a <u>great fear of contamination</u> such as germs, so they <u>repeat to wash their hands</u>.，因為害怕感染，所以不斷重複洗手，文中並未提及選項 (C) keep laughing 不停地笑，答案是 (C)。

04. **(A)** 第四題問哪個選項是公認有效的治療方式，文章提到行為療法是最有效的（But it has been accepted that behavioral therapy can be an effective treatment for OCD.）所以答案是 (A) Behavioral therapy。

05. **(B)** 文章中寫道 Nowadays OCD is diagnosed <u>nearly as common as asthma and diabetes.</u>，所以答案是 (B) as common as diabetes。

必學詞彙

> **livelihood**
> **n.** 生活；生計

> **highly processed**
> **adj.** 經過特殊加工的

> **obesity n.** 肥胖；過胖

> **migratory**
> **adj.** 遷徙的；流浪的

> **community**
> **n.** 社區；共同社會

> **increasingly**
> **adv.** 漸增地；越來越多地

> **transformation**
> **n.** 變化；轉變；變形

文法觀念

1. <u>Most of these sufferers do not enact or like these aggressive ideas, but are frustrated by some sexual, religious or vicious impulses and the fact that they **may** inexplicably harm someone.</u>

   • May 是助動詞，後方接原形動詞，用來表達「可能、或許」的意思，例：She may not be the most beautiful girl in the world, but she is the most beautiful girl to me. 她或許不是世界上最美的女孩，但她是我心中最美麗的女孩。

2. <u>The treatment for OCD can be rigorous, and the patients must be motivated with strong conviction. Using ERP, a patient can be completely **symptom free**.</u>

- Symptom free 是一組詞，-free 的用法很廣泛，其它常見有 alcohol-free（無酒精），前方幾乎可以加上任何名詞來表達「不含……、未出現……」，例句：She longs for a simple, stress-free life. 她渴望過著簡單、沒有壓力的生活。

中文翻譯

強迫症

　　對很多人來說，貝克漢是一個超級職業足球明星，他迷人的微笑和時尚風格也是廣為人知的。然而，沒有多少人知道貝克漢一直在對抗著強迫症─知名度排名第四的心理障礙。強迫症可能涉及產生焦慮的侵入性思維，想減輕焦慮地重複性行動，以及結合執著與強迫行為的舉動。強迫症患者經常做出強迫性的動作以尋求紓解跟執著有關的焦慮。一種相對模糊的執著可能意味著一種混亂感，伴隨著當生活出現不平衡時所產生的情緒威脅。例如：許多強迫症患者極度恐懼像是細菌那樣的致污物，因此他們會反覆地洗手。而那些受更嚴重執著所苦的人，可能會內心被想要以暴力傷害他人或自己的想法給占據。這些患者大部分不喜歡這些負面的念頭也不會付諸行動，但是卻會對一些性、宗教或惡意的衝動，以及他們可能會不明所以地傷害某人，為這個事實感到灰心喪氣。強迫症的症狀既是可能使患者疏離人群，治療也很耗時，更別提精神上和經濟上的重大損失。但是，行為療法一直被公認為能有效治療強迫症。用來使用在強迫症行為療法的技術稱為「持續性接觸刺激與預防慣性舉動」；這種療法是要逐漸學會如何容忍想要做慣性舉動的焦慮。例如：某人看到地板上有一些污點時，可以試著用布擦一次（接觸刺激），但不要來回仔細檢查地板是否乾淨（預防慣性舉動）。這個療法的下一個階段就是完全不要清理那些污點。如今，強迫症的診斷幾乎和哮喘及糖尿病一樣普遍。有強迫症的人不需要孤立自己，或是獨自忍受他人的抱怨。強迫症的治療是很嚴峻的，患者必須出於強烈的信念來接受治療。使用 ERP 療法，患者則可以完全擺脫症狀。

23

On "Video Conferencing"

Face-to-face meetings were once the only option for meeting with others. In the modern world, meetings can also be held through conference calls, video conferencing, or group e-mail. Due to technological advancements within the last few years, the format of conducting meetings has moved on to another new phase. Telepresence is an immersive meeting experience which allows a person to feel as if all meeting participants were present or to give the appearance that they were in the same location other than their true location. Rather than traveling great distances for a face-to-face meeting or changing the original schedule for an emergency meeting, telepresence offers more flexibility for business executives or meeting parties from different locations or countries. To a great extent, telepresence system brings enormous time and cost benefits by providing comprehensive and convincing stimuli that the user perceives no differences from actual presence. A good telepresence system puts the human factors first. By focusing on visual collaboration solutions that closely duplicate the brain's innate preferences for interpersonal communications, telepresence separates itself from the unnatural "talking heads" experience of traditional videoconferencing. The new technologies used in telepresence systems generate life-size view of participants, fluid motion, accurate flesh tones and the appearance of true eye contact. These systems include equipment such as multiple microphones, speakers, high-definition monitors, cameras, dedicated networks, and custom-made studios. So far technology has changed theways of business communication beyond our imagination. Telepresence has been used to establish a sense of shared presence and shared space among geographically separated members of a group, but how will telepresence evolve in the next decade? In June 2006 at the Networkers Conference, the chief executive officer of Cisco Systems, John Chambers compared telepresence to teleporting from Star Trek. It probably won't go that far yet. However, the design of a conference system that includes a three-dimensional image is now in progress. A 3D sensation will certainly help virtual business meetings more vivid and interactive. Are you ready for walking around other meeting participants who are actually physically hundreds of miles away from you?

___ 01. According to the passage, which sentence is not right about telepresence?
   (A) It can offer more flexibility for business executives or meeting parties.
   (B) It can bring enormous time and cost benefits.
   (C) It can allow a person to feel as if all meeting participants were absent.
   (D) It can give the appearance that the participants were in the same location.

___ 02. A good telepresence system puts _____ in the first place.
   (A) technology   (B) human   (C) distance   (D) machine

___ 03. Which equipment is included in the systems?
   (A) Multiple microphones   (B) Dedicated networks
   (C) Custom-made studios   (D) All of the above

解題技巧

1. <u>抓主題句</u> 掌握主題句最快的方式就是抓主詞跟動詞，可以很粗略的知道這篇文章的方向為何。

↳ 主題句：

> Due to technological advancements within the last few years, <u>the format of conducting meetings</u> has <u>moved on to another new phase</u>.

抓頭

▼ 關鍵字：

① 主詞：the format of conducting meetings
② 動詞：moved on to another new phase.

在這篇文章中，從主題句可掌握的是會議進行方式進入新階段。

▼ 其他資訊：

technological advancements 補充說明進入新階段是來自於科技發展。

2. <u>抓末段重點</u> 了解第一段後快速掃描最後一段，因為最後一段是結尾，看完最後一段的主題句就可以粗略了解文章的走向。

抓尾

↳ 主題句：

> However, <u>the design of a conference system</u> that includes a three-dimensional image is now in progress.

▼ 關鍵字：the design of a conference system

文章末段提到 3D 影像的會議系統目前在開發中。

補強

3. **抓各段的主題句：**

↳ 主題句：

> So far <u>technology</u> has changed the ways of business communication beyond our imagination.

▼ 關鍵字：technology

這裡在講科技澈底改變了企業溝通的方式，同樣能看出文章主題是科技進步帶來了新的會議方式。

 解析

01. **(C)** 第一題問根據文章，下列何者是錯的，文章中寫道 Telepresence is an immersive meeting experience which <u>allows a person to feel as if all meeting participants were present</u>，因此，選項 (C) It can allow a person to feel as if all meeting participants were <u>absent</u>. 為誤。

02. **(B)** 文章中寫道 A good telepresence system puts the <u>human factors</u> first. 所以答案是 (B) human。

03. **(D)** 第三題問系統裡包含哪些裝備，文章中寫道 These systems include equipment such as <u>multiple microphones</u>, speakers, high-definition monitors, cameras, <u>dedicated networks, and custom-made studios</u>. ，所以答案是 (D) All of the above。

必學詞彙

» **immersive** adj. 身歷其境的	» **innate** adj. 與生俱來的;天生的
» **participant** n. 關係者;參與者	» **physically** adv. 按照自然規律;實際上
» **stimulus** n. 刺激;刺激品	» **establish** v. 建立;設立
» **comprehensive** adj. 廣泛的;無所不包的	

文法觀念

1. Face-to-face meetings were once the only option for meeting with others.

   - Once 在這裡當成副詞,是「曾經」的意思,once 這樣用的時候,通常會擺在句子中間,例:Sarah was once my best friend, but we no longer talk. 莎拉曾是我最要好的朋友,但我們不再聯絡了。

2. So far technology has changed the ways of business communication **beyond** our imagination.

   - Beyond 是個常見的介系詞,意思是「超越」,現代常看到 ...beyondme 的用法,例:How she could treat a baby so violently is beyond me. 她竟能如此暴力地對待小嬰兒,我完全無法理解(超越我的理解範圍)。

談「視訊會議」

面對面的會議曾經是開會唯一的選擇。在現代化的世界，開會可以透過電話會議、視訊會議或是群體郵件來舉行。由於最近這幾年的科技發展，執行會議的形式已經進入到另一個新的階段了。視訊會議是一種擬真的會議經驗，可以讓所有與會人士都在同一個地點開會的感覺。與其長途旅行來參加一場面對面的會議，或是為了一個緊急會議更改原定計畫，視訊會議為來自不同地方或國家的企業執行者或會議當事者提供了更多的彈性。視訊會議在很大的程度上，帶來極大的時間及成本效益；它能提供全方位的體驗，讓使用者完全感覺不到它跟實際出席會議有什麼不同。一個良好的視訊會議系統會以人的因素擺在第一位。透過集中於複製人類大腦天生對人際溝通偏好方式的協同運作，視訊會議系統與傳統視訊會議中會出現不自然的臉部特寫有所區別。使用在視訊會議系統的新科技，能等比例顯示與會者的影像、流暢的手勢動作、精確的臉部色調以及真正的眼神接觸。這些系統包含的設備有多聲道麥克風、揚聲器、高解析度的螢幕、攝影機、精密的網路以及定製的錄音室。目前科技已經超乎我們想像地改變了企業溝通的方式。視訊會議被用來打破群體間彼此地理位置的分隔限制，但是往後十年，視訊會議又將如何發展呢？在2006年六月的網路工作者會議中，思科系統的執行長約翰・錢博將遠距會議與「星際爭霸戰」中的全相投影技術做了一番比較。視訊會議可能不會發展到那種地步，不過，3D 影像的會議系統目前已經在開發中。3D 的影像無疑地會讓商務會議更顯得生動及有互動感。你是否已經準備好要在實際上離你有好幾百哩遠的會議夥伴身邊走動了呢？

24

The Good Negotiation Skill

Any aggressive company leaders who run successful and prestigious business in their own countries would naturally aim to extend their successful domestic experience to the international setting. Yet, they may have difficulty achieving the goal if they fail in building successful international business relationships in their international business negotiations, which are basically different from domestic negotiations and require different knowledge and skills. Cultural differences can be barriers to simple communications in any international business meetings. Different languages, values, perceptions, and philosophies can make simple conversation complicated. A key word during any cross-cultural communication might not be translated correctly due to different cultural backgrounds. Thus, delegating a competent representative to undertake such assignment should give a better starting point. In order to bridge the language and cultural gap, the representatives must listen closely and carefully. Instead of focusing on cultural differences during negotiations, concentrate on mutual interests and nurturing long-term relationships. In the international marketplace, having the capability of negotiating with cross-culture business is crucial to success without any exception. Whenever you are involved in global negotiations or international conferences, keep in mind that you might be working with the same person for the next few decades. Negotiations should involve creating value for all parties. Try creating win-win outcomes for all parties during negotiations. Negotiations should be straightforward and open, because they are important moments when trust is being established and verified. Be honest and state your desires clearly. Listen, understand and evaluate what your business partner is requesting with caution. Be sure of what you are negotiating and agreeing to. Consent to what you cannot perform or achieve under no circumstance. Prepare for the meeting several weeks ahead. Refresh and add information daily before it happens so that you will be in control of the information and feel confident during the meeting. Last but not least, any agreement must have complete follow-through. If any problem occurs in the follow-through, immediately contact and communicate the situation to your partner.

___ 01. According to the passage, which sentence is not right about international business?
   (A) Building successful international business relationship is very important.
   (B) It might be not so easy for one to establish an international business.
   (C) It is basically different from domestic negotiations.
   (D) It requires the same knowledge and skills of domestic negotiations.

___ 02. _____ can make a simple conversation complicated.
   (A) different perceptions and philosophies
   (B) different languages
   (C) different values
   (D) A, B and C

___ 03. In order to bridge the language and cultural gap, the representatives are not supposed to _____.
(A) listen closely and carefully
(B) concentrate on mutual interests
(C) focus on cultural differences
(D) nurture long-term relationships

 解題技巧 ─────────────────────────

1. **抓主題句** 掌握主題句最快的方式就是抓主詞跟動詞,可以很粗略的知道這篇文章的方向為何。

↳ 主題句:

> In the international marketplace, having the capability of negotiating with cross-culture business is crucial to success without any exception.

抓頭

▼ 關鍵字:

① 主詞:the international marketplace
② 動詞:having the capability of negotiating
在這篇文章中,從主題句可以掌握的是國際市場和談判能力。

▼ 其他資訊:with cross-culture business
補充說明在跨國貿易情況下。

2. **抓末段重點** 了解第一段後快速掃描最後一段,因為最後
一段是結尾,看完最後一段的主題句就可以
粗略了解文章的走向。

抓尾

↳ 主題句:

> If any problem occurs in the follow-through, immediately
> contact and communicate the situation to your partner.

▼ 關鍵字:communicate

文章末段提到溝通,同樣能看出文章與企業之間的溝通
有關。

補強

3. **抓各段的主題句**:

↳ 主題句:

> Try creating win-win outcomes for all parties during
> negotiations.

▼ 關鍵字:negotiations

文章建議試著利用談判能力創造雙贏局面,由此看出文
章主題。

 解析

01. **(D)** 第一題問根據文章,下列何者為誤,文章中提到
國內談判和跨國談判不一樣,因此,答案是 (D)
It requires the same knowledge and skills of domestic
negotiations.。

02. **(D)** 第二題問哪些因素能讓溝通變得困難,文章
中寫道 Different languages, values, perceptions,
and philosophies can make simple conversation
complicated.,所以答案是 (D) A, B and C。

03. **(C)** 第三題問代表人在談判過程中該怎麼做，文章中寫道 <u>Instead of focusing on cultural differences during negotiations, concentrate on mutual interests and nurturing long-term relationships.</u> 所以答案是 (C) focus on cultural differences。

 **必學詞彙**

» **aggressive**
　adj. 有進取精神的；
　　　有幹勁的

» **prestigious**
　adj. 有名望的

» **negotiation**
　n. 談判；協商

» **representative n.** 典型；代表物；代表

» **straightforward**
　adj. 老實的；坦率的

» **immediately**
　adv. 立即；即刻；馬上

» **circumstance**
　n. 情況；環境；事件

 文法觀念

1. <u>Yet, they may have difficulty achieving the goal if they fail in building successful international business relationships in their international business negotiations, which are basically different from domestic negotiations, and require different knowledge and skills.</u>

- Yet 是「然而」的意思，可放句首，也可放句中，例：She forgives him, yet she couldn't stay with him. 她原諒了他，但無法繼續和他在一起。放句尾時，通常有不同的意思（還未），例：I haven't finished my work yet. 我的工作還沒有做完。

2. <u>Consent to what you cannot perform or achieve under nocircumstance.</u>

    - Under 是「在……之下」的意思，可以是實際的，也可以指形式上的，例：Amy works very well under pressure. 艾咪在壓力下工作，表現得很好。

 **中文翻譯**

良好的談判技巧

　　任何在國內經營公司成功、富企業聲望，並具企圖心的企業領導人，會自然地以他們在國內成功的經驗拓展到國際環境中為目標。然而，他們如果無法在國際商務談判中建立成功的國際商務關係，要達成這個目標就很困難，因為國際商務談判基本上與國內談判是不同的，需要不同的知識和技巧。文化差異在任何國際商務會議中可能會是簡單溝通的障礙。不同的語言、價值觀及想法會使簡單的溝通變得複雜。在任何一個跨文化的溝通中，一個關鍵字可能會因為不同的文化背景而無法被準確地翻譯出來；因此，委派能勝任代表的人來進行任務，應該是個好的開始。為了縮短語言以及文化隔閡，代表人必須仔細聆聽。與其將重心放在文化差異上，倒不如全神貫注於共同利益以及培養長期關係上。在國際市場上，擁有能夠與跨文化

企業協商談判的能力，毫無例外地會是成功的關鍵。當你參加
國際協商或國際會議時，都要記住你可能會跟同一個人一起合
作好幾十年。協商內容必須與為各方創造價值有關。試著在協
商中創造雙贏的結果。協商過程必須直接且公開。會議是兩方
確立信任關係的重要時刻，要誠實並且清楚地聲明你的要求；
聆聽、理解並且審慎地評估事業夥伴的請求。確定你要協商的
內容和同意的事項；無論在任何情況下，都不要答應你無法做，
或是無法達成的事。會議前幾週就著手準備，在會議之前隨時
更新並補充資訊，如此一來，在溝通的過程中你就能掌握所有
資訊並且充滿自信。最後很重要的一點，在會議中協定的事項
都必須確實執行；若是執行中發生任何問題，立刻與對方取得
聯繫並做溝通。

25

The Real Heaven

An old man and his dog were walking along a country road, enjoying the pleasant scenery. The man soon became aware that he was actually dead, and his dog had been dead for many years. The two walked in silence and wondered where the journey would lead them. After a long walk, their legs became heavy as if they were going to drop from exhaustion. Suddenly the dog barked in excitement as there was a magnificent gate standing before them. The old man believed that they finally arrived at heaven. As the man and the dog got closer to the gate, they saw someone sitting in front of the gate. The old man then called out, "Excuse me. Is this heaven?" "Yes, it is, sir. You look weary. Come right in, and I will give you some water and food." The gatekeeper replied, and the gate began to open. Just when the man and the dog were about to enter, the gatekeeper pointed at the dog and said, "I'm sorry, sir, but we don't accept pets." The man contemplated the gate in despair and decided to turn back toward the road. Once again, the two continued their journey together. After another long walk, they came to a dirt road that led through a farm gate. The gate was worn-out and there was no fence. "Excuse me!" the old man called to the person who was sitting inside the gate. "May I have some water?" "Sure, come on in. There is plenty of water and food." "How about my friend here?" the old man gestured to his dog. "He's welcome too," the gatekeeper replied in such a delightful voice. After drinking, the old man asked the gatekeeper, "What do you call this place?" "This is heaven," the gatekeeper answered calmly. "But the man sitting in front of the magnificent gate said that place was heaven," the old man said. "No, that's hell, and it actually saves us a lot of time by screening out the people who would leave their best friends behind," said the gatekeeper.

___ 01. About the story, which one of the following is not correct?
  (A) it happened in reality   (B) it involves an old man and a dog
  (C) they found heaven finally   (D) they departed the hell

___ 02. Why did the dog bark suddenly in excitement?
  (A) the dog saw food   (B) the dog saw a magnificent gate
  (C) the dog was too hungry   (D) the dog was too tired

___ 03. At the rst time, the gatekeeper didn't allow the dog in because they didn't accept _____.
  (A) human   (B) friends   (C) pigs   (D) pets

___ 04. At the end of the story, the farm gate that they came to turned out to be _____.
  (A) hell   (B) heaven   (C) farmland   (D) factory

___ 05. What do you think is the most important quality of the old man that probably made him got to the heaven finally?
  (A) selfishness   (B) shamelessness
  (C) kindness   (D) betrayal

解題技巧

1. **抓主題句** 掌握主題句最快的方式就是抓主詞跟動詞，可以很粗略的知道這篇文章的方向為何。

↳ 主題句：

> An old man and his dog were walking along a country road, enjoying the pleasant scenery.

▼ 關鍵字：

① 主詞：An old man and his dog　② 動詞：walking

在這篇文章中，從主題句可以掌握的是老人與狗在散步。

▼ 其他資訊：

→ a country road 是補充說明老人與狗走在鄉村小路上。

2. **抓末段重點** 了解第一段後快速掃描最後一段，因為最後一段是結尾，看完最後一段的主題句就可以粗略了解文章的走向。

↳ 主題句：

> After drinking, the old man asked the gatekeeper, "What do you call this place?" "This is heaven," the gatekeeper answered calmly.

▼ 關鍵字：heaven

文章末段提到天堂，得知老人最後找到了真正的天堂。

抓頭

抓尾

3. **抓各段的主題句：**

↳ 主題句：

> The man contemplated the gate in despair and decided to turn back toward the road.

▼ 關鍵字：turn back

老人決定往回走，這是文章中的重點，老人決定帶著狗往回走，最後找到了真正的天堂。

解析

01. **(A)** 第一題問哪個選項是錯誤的，這是一個虛構的故事，所以答案是 (A) it happened in reality。

02. **(B)** 第二題問小狗為什麼興奮地狂吠，文章中寫道 Suddenly the dog barked in excitement as there was a magnificent gate standing before them.，可見答案是 (B) the dog saw a magnificent gate。

03. **(D)** 第三題問第一次看門者為何不讓他們進去，文章中寫道 the gatekeeper pointed at the dog and said, I'm sorry, sir, but we don't accept pets.",所以答案是 (D) pets。

04. **(B)** 第四題問他們最終進入什麼地方，老人與狗離開第一個地方，因為那裡不接受寵物，到了第二個地方時，看門者說他們來到了天堂，答案是 (B) heaven。

05. **(C)** 第五題問哪一項特質讓老人上了天堂，看完故事後，可知老人並沒有為了上天堂而拋棄寵物，答案應是 (C) kindness。

 **必學詞彙**

> **journey**
> n. 旅程；旅行；行程

> **exhaustion**
> n. 耗盡；枯竭；精疲
> 力竭

> **contemplate**
> v. 深思熟慮；注視

> **gatekeeper** n. 看門人；守門員；門神

> **despair** n. 絕望

> **delightful**
> adj. 令人愉快的；令人
> 高興的

> **magnificent**
> adj. 豪華的；華麗的

 文法觀念

1. <u>As the man and the dog got closer to the gate, they saw someone sitting in front of the gate.</u>

   • As 在這裡是「當……時」的意思，可擺句首或句尾，例：
   As I sat down on the chair, the cat jump on to my lap. 當我在椅子上坐下時，貓咪就跳到了我的腿上。

2. <u>"No, that's hell, and it actually saves us a lot of time by screening out the people who would **leave** their best friends **behind**,"</u> said <u>the gatekeeper.</u>

   • Behind 原本是「在……之後」的意思，前面加上 leave 就成了片語，leave...behind 是很常見的片語，例：Her father left the whole family behind for another woman. 她父親為了別的女人拋棄全家人。

真正的天堂

　　一個老翁和他的狗沿著鄉村小路散步,享受著沿途的怡人風景。老翁隨即意識到自己實際上已經死了,而他的狗也已經死了很多年。老人與狗在沉默中走著,猜想這段旅程會帶他們到哪裡去。在走了好長一段路之後,他們的腳變得好沉重,他們似乎就要因疲累而倒下了。忽然間那隻狗興奮地狂吠,因為就在他們面前,矗立著一座華麗的大門。老翁相信他們終於來到了天堂了。就在老人與狗更走近大門時,他們看到有人坐在大門的前面。老翁於是喊了:「請問一下,這裡是天堂嗎?」「是的,沒錯。你看起來很疲倦呢。快進來!我拿些水和食物給你。」看門者回答,接著大門就打開了。就在老人與狗要進入之時,看門者指著狗説:「先生,不好意思。寵物不得進入。」老人絕望地凝視著大門,並決定要轉身走回原路。再次地,老人與狗一起繼續他們的旅程。又走了好一段路之後,他們來到一條通往農場大門的泥路。那個大門破爛不堪,而且也沒有藩籬。「打擾了!」老人對著坐在大門裡的人喊著:「我可以喝點水嗎?」「當然啊,進來吧。這兒有很多的水和食物。」「那我的朋友呢?」老人比著他的狗。「也歡迎他進來。」看門者以高興的聲音回答。喝了水之後,老人問看門者:「這是什麼地方?」看門者冷靜地答道:「這裡是天堂。」「不過坐在那座華麗大門前的人説那裡是天堂耶。」老人説。「不,那裡是地獄,而事實上那裡幫我們省了很多時間,替我們過濾掉那些棄自己最好的朋友不顧的人。」看門者回答。

語研力 E095

征服考場 英文閱讀得分王：用「抓補法」速效解題技巧，戰勝克漏字及閱讀測驗！

作　　者	Michael Yang
顧　　問	曾文旭
出版總監	陳逸祺、耿文國
主　　編	陳蕙芳
執行編輯	翁芯琍
美術編輯	李依靜
法律顧問	北辰著作權事務所

印　　製	世和印製企業有限公司
初　　版	2024 年 05 月
出　　版	凱信企業集團 - 凱信企業管理顧問有限公司
電　　話	（02）2773-6566
傳　　真	（02）2778-1033
地　　址	106 台北市大安區忠孝東路四段 218 之 4 號 12 樓
信　　箱	kaihsinbooks@gmail.com

定　　價	新台幣 349 元 / 港幣 116 元
產品內容	1 書

總 經 銷	采舍國際有限公司
地　　址	235 新北市中和區中山路二段 366 巷 10 號 3 樓
電　　話	（02）8245-8786
傳　　真	（02）8245-8718

國家圖書館出版品預行編目資料

征服考場 英文閱讀得分王：用「抓補法」速效
解題技巧，戰勝克漏字及閱讀測驗！／Michael
Yang 著. – 初版. – 臺北市：凱信企業集團凱信企
業管理顧問有限公司, 2024.05
　　面；　公分
ISBN 978-626-7354-39-1(平裝)

1.CST: 英語　2.CST: 讀本

805.1892　　　　　　　　　　　113001948